THE '40 FORD TITANIUM CAMSHAFT

A prequel story for
The Bootlegger '40 Ford

Charles S. Clark
FLATHEAD PRESS LLC

2017 © by Charles S. Clark.
All rights reserved.

This is a work of fiction. Names, characters, places and incidents are the product of the author's imagination or are used fictitiously, and any resemblance to actual persons, living or dead, events or locales, is entirely coincidental. The names of actual persons are used by permission.

Portions of this material also appear on the
author's website, www.CharlesSClarkAuthor.com
© by Charles S. Clark. All rights reserved.

No part of this book may be reproduced or transmitted in any form or by any means, electronic or mechanical, including photocopying, recording, or by any information storage and retrieval system, without permission in writing from the publisher.
For information address: Flathead Press, www.CharlesSClarkAuthor.com

Story and Dialogue Consultant: Mara Purl
Copy Editor: Peggy Ireland
Interior designer: Rebecca Finkel, F + P Graphic Design
Cover design: Nick Zelinger, NZ Graphics

ISBN (print) 978-0-9903526-5-5

ISBN (eBook) 978-0-9903526-7-9

ISBN (audio) 978-0-9903526-8-6

Wanted to let you know I THOROUGHLY enjoyed it! Thanks so much for giving it to us. I have a list of people I am passing it on to, starting with LCOC President Talbourdet Also, could you email me some information on the outfit that put the gold plating on the hood ornament of your '41?

—*Steve D'Ambrosia*,
LCOC (Lincoln Continental Owners Club) National Chief Judge

"*A hot-rod adventure? Not my cup of tea? So I thought, until I read* The Bootlegger '40 Ford. *Now I'd say Charles S. Clark's stories are my cup of molten java! His stories are brainy enough to give you the inner workings of complex, high-performance machines, but it's the vulnerability of his characters that tug at your heartstrings. I was honored when he asked if characters in his new story could visit my fictional town of Milford-Haven. I hope they return again and again, just as I will, to his excellent writing.*"

—*Mara Purl*,
best-selling author of The Milford-Haven Novels

Praise for *The Bootlegger '40 Ford*

Thank you for sending me your book, The Bootlegger '40 Ford. *I really enjoyed each chapter and appreciate the detail and story lines.*

—*Ray Everham*
Ray Everham Enterprises, LLC
Three time Winston Cup Series Champion with driver Jeff Gordon

Okay gear-head wives, here's your chance to get your gear-head guy into reading books! Order this book now, and put it away for his birthday, anniversary, or that other special day. Even if he's not a reader, the cover art and much more by Darrell Mayabb, a name he will recognize right off, will suck him into this great read from the very imaginative mind of new writer Charles Clark. Clark has a remarkable knowledge of the fabulous Ford Flathead engine, and can tell a fictional story as if he was actually there, even if he does have to make a lot of it up. Your guy will keep the pages turning as soon as he discovers the accuracy of the technical details. In my 20 years as a contributing editor for most of the popular street rodding magazines, it is refreshing not to read terms such as a 1932 Ford Deuce, or a '40 Ford five window coupe.

—*Dave Hill*

I would go full steam ahead toward a movie using every contact you can find. You have a good product and you ought to be sure all auto lovers read it!

—*Philip Bueth*
Past President of the ABC Network's *Good Morning America*

Introduction

The history of the United States of America is replete with tales of strong men and women and their self-reliance and perseverance in the face of difficulty. Nothing was assured. If you wanted to eat, you grew your own crops. If you had problems, you solved them. If you had a family, you cared for them. The government was not there to provide for you. You had to provide for yourself.

Along with the growth of the population came the growth of big government. The pace of industry and social progress made it essential that laws be created that governed how society would interact in a controlled manner. Someone had to pay for all this government service and thus we have taxation. In the United States taxation has always been thought of as a voluntary obligation which the citizenship imposes on itself rather than being mandated by the King of England as occurred before the Revolution.

However when the laws regarding taxation run into established customs the result is tax evasion. If a segment of the population feels they are being taxed unjustly or just plain do not want to pay the tax then conflict between the people and the government results. Such is the case with the tax on alcohol, one of the country's oldest taxes. The imposition of this tax led to the creation in early times of the "Bootlegger." He was a liquor tax evasion specialist who distilled and sold liquor without paying taxes. To evade the tax collector in the early days, he would hide his illegal brew in his high-top leather boots.

As the industrial revolution led to the manufacture of automobiles that the average worker could afford, they became the natural successor to the horse-riding bootleggers for the transportation and sale of illegal untaxed whiskey. The southeastern United States was the hotbed of this activity and it was where the technology of using the automobile for bootlegging was developed into a fine homespun art.

Research and first-hand information are the foundation of my stories, though I do take creative license as needed in the weaving of my tales. I dwell on the character of real people in my stories—people I know and respect and who have helped me gain knowledge and experience on how to build a hot rod and do car restorations.

Such a person is Jerry Price the owner of Draggin the Ave Customs in Castle Rock, Colorado. Jerry and his wife Rose enter this story as the main characters where they behave as they might have as early residents of Boone, North Carolina. The fantastic 1940 Ford coupe that you encounter still exists today. Thank you Jerry and Rose for the use of your names.

Join me, now, as we follow their fictional personnas and other Appalachian families that were part of this amazing bootlegging phenomenon. You can read about the adventures that they initiated in *The Bootlegger '40 Ford,* the first novel in my series. And by the way, one of the Price family's fantastic vehicles still exists today.

—Charles S. Clark

New Year's Day in Boone

The sound of the explosion was deafening. New Year's Day, 1920 was literally starting with a bang, thanks to Walter Price and his brother Jerry. They'd hefted an anvil out of Jerry's blacksmith shop, put a stick of dynamite under it, and blown it fifty feet in the air. All one hundred seventy-nine citizens of this small North Carolina town—named after the great Daniel Boone—far from being terrified by the sound, knew it signified a joyous event: the addition of one new member of their community.

The Appalachian hill town was happy to have something to celebrate as a new year dawned, and Walter, more than anyone, was jubilant when he learned his wife Sally had given birth to a baby boy.

But by five that afternoon, word had already spread like wildfire through the village, and as the sun descended over the mountains, the town sank into quiet despair. Sally Price had died in childbirth.

The ten-year-old boy—who'd been named for his uncle—stared through the smoked glasses, mesmerized by the bright light of the welding torch. It'd been more than a year since he'd started his unofficial apprenticeship and already he'd learned enough about blacksmithing that he could shape the horseshoes his uncle made for customers. But he'd also been experimenting with the cutting and welding torches, listening as the metal began to whisper to him. He loved how it crackled when he cut, and sizzled when he welded, and his diligent learning was making him an expert at a very young age.

Life was good now. His aunt and uncle had made him feel that he had a real home when they adopted him. He'd never known his mom. And he didn't remember his dad much anymore. He knew that, after his mom had died, his father Walter had moved to Charlotte to take a job in the asbestos factory making fireproof coating for industrial buildings. He'd tended to baby Jerr as best he could but had to leave him much of the time with a wonderful black mammy named Sapphire. Sometimes he remembered hearing her voice when she sang him to sleep. Then, when he'd been five years old, his father had died. He'd heard some of the grownups say it was lung cancer due to exposure to the asbestos fibers, but he didn't really understand what that meant. All he knew was that with his father's death he'd become an orphan. Despite this, he'd never felt truly alone or unloved. His dad's brother Jerry and his wife Marge brought him into their home to take care of him. To the village Uncle Jerry and his nephew became known as Big Jerr and Little Jerr and Little Jerr was delighted by that.

Little Jerr goes to the one room schoolhouse where he's already learned to read and write and do figures. He knows Big Jerr has his best interest at heart, and he's also figured out that his uncle is having a difficult time making a living as a blacksmith in the local farm community, so he works long hours. Partly to help, and partly because he likes it so much, Little Jerr spends his time away from school in the blacksmith shop. He watches his uncle as he heats steel wagon wheel rims red hot in the forge and then hammer welds them together. As soon as he can manage, he's given the task of working the bellows for the forge. He gets to see the iron wheel rims and horse shoes turn red hot and then see how they can be shaped and joined by Big Jerr's powerful hammer blows on the steel anvil that ring out like shots being fired.

Big Jerr's smart—everyone says so—and he becomes one of the first hill blacksmiths to adopt acetylene welding. This helps grow his business as he can now do more complicated jobs. Little Jerr loves everything about how Big Jerr lets him experiment, except for one day when he got a harsh lesson. Some hot sparks flew off and burned a hole through his pants. It hurt really badly, and even worse when Aunt Marge put medicine on the burn. From then on, he was gonna' wrap his arms and legs in deer hide.

Time For Some Fun

It's not all work and no play in the village. Once a month as weather permits they push the old fire wagon out of the fire house, hang up a white bed sheet for a screen, and show movies. The women make a big pot of hunter's stew on the old cast iron stove. They use fresh vegetables from the garden and venison from the smoke house. Often a little possum is thrown in to kick up the flavor.

The menfolk uncork a brown jug of white lightening whiskey that they brewed and pass it around. Little Jerr sneaks a gulp and gags as the powerful brew goes down his throat. Big Jerr has to turn away and laugh when he sees that. Well, the boy has to learn some time, he figures.

When it gets dark they fire up the electric generator and turn on the projector. Little Jerr is mesmerized when the film of the Brooklands race track in England comes on the screen. He sees the German Blitzen Benz racer going 127 mph around the track setting a world record. Its huge 21 liter engine shooting flames out of its four exhaust pipes as big as sewer pipes. He can only imagine the sound of that monster engine as he sees it leave a trail of exhaust smoke as it flies around the track. He knows that someday he will go that fast. It becomes his goal in life.

The Hard Lessons

The sound of the ohgah horn and some flying dust announce the arrival of Bill Kelly, the smiling Irish hardware drummer man from Raleigh. He climbs out of his Model T, his duster coat covered in dirt, and pulls the goggles off his head. Bill is well known as he comes around about once a month to take tool and hardware orders from the farmers. His 1925 Model T Ford sounds real funny; it is not running right. Bending over the fender, he opens the side panel of the engine and he and Big Jerr stick their heads down close to the running engine and listen to it misfire.

Big Jerr shakes his head and remarks, "She sounds a little sick, Bill."

"Oh, she's a dilly when she runs right but started frettin' coming over the grade into town. Not sure that she'll make it to Raleigh."

"Well, better leave it here and take the bus back. I'll see if I can fix it for you. Should have it ready in a week. Takes that long to get parts in from Charlotte."

"I guess I'm hog-tied till then. Do the best that you can."

Big Jerr is right up-to-date on the Model T. He had gone to a special school in Charlotte put on by a Ford factory mechanic and learned how to repair them.

Little Jerr is totally excited. He's going to see how a car works. First thing in the morning Big Jerr starts working on the car with Little Jerr looking right over his shoulder. Big Jerr has to brush the boy's head to one side. He's just so excited to see what is going on.

"Looks like the trembler coil is shot and the plugs are fouled. No tin Lizzie is going to run with that kind of problem," he declares.

"How does the air and gas get inside the engine? Why doesn't it just go through without doing anything?" Little Jerr asks as he looks intently at the engine.

"Jerr, I am going to explain how an engine works in a way that you can actually feel. We are going to play a little game. Now think of your left hand as being the intake valve that lets air into the engine and your right hand as the exhaust valve that lets air out of the engine. Your lungs are now the combustion chamber where air-fuel mixture burns to drive the piston which in turn causes the car to move. Ready for the game?"

Jerr pulls his head out from under the hood of the Model T and stands straight up eager to play the game.

"OK, put your left hand over your mouth and pinch your nose closed with the right hand. See how no air can get in or out? That is the situation with both valves closed."

Jerr is holding his breath and starts to feel his lungs getting tight.

"Now take your left hand away and breathe deep. That is the intake valve coming open."

Jerr feels his lungs fill with much needed air.

"Now close the 'intake valve' and trap the air so you imagine that it is the gas burning inside the combustion chamber."

Jerr feels the air trapped inside his lungs as they start to *burn*.

"Now stop pinching your nose with your right hand and let the trapped air in your lungs go out. That is the exhaust valve getting rid of the burned gas."

Both of them giggle a little at the silly game they are playing. Little Jerr keeps doing the exercise with his two hands. It is a really funny way to breathe.

"OK, now we are going to do something a little different. Open the 'intake valve,' your mouth, and start to take a breath but quickly close it. Do the same with the 'exhaust valve,' your nose."

Little Jerr does as he's told and starts snorting as he takes the partial breaths.

"See that's not a good way to breathe. If you tried to run breathing like that you would not go very fast or very far because you would run out of gas."

Little Jerr starts running in a circle whooping and snorting as he does the funny exercise but has to stop after just two circles of the T because he's laughing so hard.

"So now maybe you can understand not only how the intake and exhaust valves work but also how important it is to have them open and close at the right time so the engine can make the most power. That is the job of the camshaft. It opens and closes the valves at exactly the right time. You can think of it as the heart of the engine."

"Oh yes, yes! I get what's going on inside an engine now." His face is beaming with the excitement of the new knowledge that he has so loving obtained from his uncle.

"I love engines," Little Jerr says as he gives his uncle a big smile. "Someday I am going to make my own engine."

"Well, that's a great idea but you have a lot to learn so pay attention in school."

It takes four days to get the new coil from Charlotte. While he's at it he also gets some new clutch material because he knows that'll be the next problem. With the new coil installed and the wool clutch replaced she's ready to roll. Big Jerr inserts the crank in the nose of the T, gives it a big yank and the four cylinder engine springs to life with the "ah to at to wah" sound that is so well known to tin Lizzie drivers.

"Hop in, Jerr, let's take her for a spin."

This is Little Jerr's first time in a car. Jumping with excitement, he hops into the black button-leather seat right beside his uncle. He presses his feet against the firewall and pushes his hands into the hard leather. The sun-heated leather burns his bare legs that are not covered by his short pants. He lifts his legs into the air to stop the pain. Big Jerr presses the left pedal that puts the transmission in gear and off they go in a cloud of dust down the road. On the straight stretch he kicks it up to 35 miles per hour, and the big windshield vibrates as the tires skip over the ruts.

"She's a runner for sure now," Big Jerr declares as they pull into the shop driveway." He goes to the back of the shop to start another job fixing a broken plow.

The temptation is too much for Little Jerr. He climbs out of the high seat and kicks up some dirt with his Keds sneakers. Walking to the front of the T, he casts his eyes on the hand crank. "I'll bet I can turn that," he tells himself. He figures it can't hurt to just try it, so he wraps both hands around the crank and gives it a pull with all his might. The engine pops and fires backward with the crank engaged and he breaks his thumb. Screaming in pain, he runs into the house to find Aunt Marge.

A month later the thumb is healed, but it still hurts. Big Jerr decides that he won't get mad at the boy, as the T gave him enough punishment. Instead, he decides to teach the boy about what caused his pain.

"First off, Jerr, you never wrap your hand around the crank. You leave your thumb off it so if it does kick back it won't hurt you. The reason that it kicked back on you is because you didn't pull down the lever on the steering wheel that retards the spark that let the spark plug fire too soon and rotate the engine backwards. The crank handle cannot disengage when it does that. You understand?"

"Yes, sir, I was stupid." He looks down at the ground and with his good thumb hooked on his belt he circles the dirt with his right foot.

"Not stupid, Jerr, just careless. You need to learn about things before you try and use them. Now I want you to start that T over there the right way."

"I'm afraid it'll hurt me again."

"No need to be a feared of it. You do it right and it cannot hurt you. It is just a machine and you can master it. Now go ahead and do it, boy."

With Big Jerr's assistance he climbs up behind the steering wheel and pulls down the spark advance lever just like he's shown how to do. He gulps hard and puts his hands around the crank with the thumbs on the outside. He winces as he pulls it hard. The T engine starts and runs. Little Jerr now has a big smile. He's learned several lessons that he will never forget.

Miss Johnson

Jerr does just fine in high school. In history class he learns about how the country was founded during the Revolutionary War and how the South was torn apart by the Civil War. He even gets to meet an old soldier who fought in that war. The legend of Daniel Boone and the early frontiersmen is drilled into him so he knows how the village got its name.

Miss Johnson, the spinster mathematics teacher, drives up from Charlotte in her Chevy coupe once a week to teach the junior and senior class. She is a nice lady but is kinda' skinny with gray hair. Jerr really likes to learn trigonometry because he can see it in his mind and it makes a lot of sense to him. It fits right in his head along with what he did with Big Jerr in the blacksmith shop and what he does in carpentry work.

Algebra is a bad subject. All the Xs, Ys and Zs make no sense to him and he's going to fail the course and perhaps not be able to graduate. Miss Johnson knows that the boy is bright but has some sort of mental block. So after class one day she stays on to tutor him.

"Jerr, can you talk?"

What a silly question Jerr thinks but he knows he has to be polite. Big Jerr gave him a whipping once when he was in fifth grade and back sassed a teacher.

"Yes, ma'am," Jerr mumbles as he looks down at the floor. Even with the windows open the schoolroom is hot and the sweat is rolling down inside his long johns. Miss Johnson looks as cool as a cucumber. Not a single strand of the gray hair knotted up on the back of her head is out of place.

"Write down what I am saying. 'John is three times older than Sue and Sue is the same age as Frank. Frank is ten years old.' Now circle the first letters in the names. Now we will write an equation using the circled letters and use an equal sign for the word "is" and the symbol "x" for the word 'times.' You do it now."

Jerr starts: John (J), is (=), 3, times (x), Sue (S). Sue (S), is (=) Frank (F). Frank (F) is (=) 10.

"Now you use the letters and symbols to make an equation with what you have written."

"$J = 3 \times S$ and $S = F$ and $F = 10$"

"So we know S equals F which is 10 so we put it in the first equation and solve that John is 30 years old. We started out talking and used symbols to replace words and made an equation. You see that?" Miss Johnson says as she peers over the bifocal glasses that are chained around her neck.

"Yes, ma'am," Jerr says as a light bulb started to go on his head. It was starting to make sense to him.

"One more thing we need to do and that is make a general equation out of our special equation. We will substitute X, Y and Z for J, S and F so we get:

$X = 3Y$ and $Y = Z$ and $Z = 10$. What is the value of X?

The answer to this question is your first homework problem."

"Oh yes, now I see what you mean about if I can talk I can do algebra. It's kinda' fun."

Miss Johnson smiles as she realizes she is launching another ship on the sea of life. That is what makes teaching worthwhile for her. Jerr doesn't know it yet but he's obtaining valuable mental tools that will set the course for his future life.

Graduation Day

School is finally over and graduation day is here at last. No more homework at night smelling the stinky kerosene lamp. No more freezing in the snow walking to school during a winter storm. It is time to celebrate. There are eight boys and five girls in the senior class. The auditorium in the small school will be filled with proud parents and close relatives. It is an occasion for the entire town to celebrate as these young people stride into the future. All the stores hang signs of congratulations in the window.

Aunt Marge had insisted that Jerr was going to look like a successful young man. She ordered a store bought coat and pants from the Sears and Roebuck catalog. It didn't quite fit right so she had cut and hemmed it until it did. Now it brings a secret tear to her eye when she sees him put it on for the first time. So tragic it is that his mother could not be here to see her grown up boy.

The night before graduation is the senior year party. They clear out the fire house and decorate it with crepe paper in the blue and gold school colors. They put peonies and lilacs in vases around the room so it gives a sweet springtime perfume smell to the building.

The girls all wear frilly skirts that they sewed and the boys wear cotton pants and white shirts with string ties. It is a celebration for the town but it is the kids turn to be happy and full of fun.

Mr. Johansson plays the fiddle and his son is on the washboard. Bill Kelly, the hardware drummer from Raleigh, stays to play the washtub git fiddle. Little Tom Warren rips away on the accordion. The happy noise fills the room and Alice and Henry jump up and start clog dancing, while the rest of the crowd clap hands for them.

Big Jerr along with some of the other men have a small bottle of shine tucked away in their pants. He lets Little Jerr have a nip. He figures he's no longer a kid and can do things that men do.

Little Jerr steps outside to get a breath of fresh air and sees Betty Sue sitting on the running board of the fire engine. He takes a deep breath and sits down beside her.

"Whew! What a night." He's a little tipsy from the powerful white lightning that he swallowed.

"Sure is, Jerr. I am just so excited. It is finally over and we are going to graduate."

Jerr has known Betty Sue since first grade. In third grade he dipped her pigtails in the ink well and she gave him a big slap in the face for that. He watched her change from a tom boy into a young woman. It was this beautiful young woman that was beside him in the bright moonlight that caused him to feel giddy in a way he had never felt before. He could see her blouse swelled with newly developed breasts.

Suddenly, they stand simultaneously and Jerr puts his arm around her. With his other hand, he gently touches her face, turning it toward him so he can kiss her. It's the first time he's ever kissed a girl this way. He can feel her soft body against him and smell the sweet perfume of her hair.

The side door of the firehouse burst open and Big Jerr strides outside.

"Oh, there you two are. Better get inside. They are starting the square dance and need another couple."

The Lecture

After the night of celebration and before the kids leave for the school and the graduation ceremony, Big Jerr asks Little Jerr to come sit with him under the big oak tree.

"Now son, what you were doing last night with Betty Sue is natural and nothing to be ashamed of. What you have to realize is that you are now a man and must be prepared to take on a man's responsibilities. When you are ready to do that you can get intimate with a woman the way that the Good Lord intended. Until that time you need to control yourself. Do you understand that?"

"Yes, I think I do. I guess I just got carried away."

"Believe me, you are far and away not the first young man that got carried away by a pretty girl in the moonlight. It is one of life's greatest pleasures. What I am saying is that it also is one of life's biggest responsibilities. You handle it like the man that I know you are and everything will be fine. Now go get the Model A while I hustle up Aunt Marge."

"I love you, Jerr. I don't know what my life would be without you and Aunt Marge."

Charlotte

Big Jerr knows that young Jerr could be a big help to him if he knew how to fix cars so he makes a deal with Frank Sims, the owner of the Ford agency in Charlotte. He would fix the well in his summer cabin if Frank would let Jerr work in the repair shop for a month.

Jerr is excited and also a little scared as he has never been away from home. Now he's about to be gone for a month and stay in a rooming house and sleep in a strange bed. This will be an all new experience for him but Aunt Marge helps him pack some clothes, tells him how to get laundry done, and what is best to order in a restaurant when he can't get a meal in Ella Bourn's boarding house. Just make sure that the food is cooked fresh she says and don't drink Moxie in place of water.

As it turns out he doesn't have time to get homesick because he's put right in the middle of learning how a car is put together. He learns how to take an engine apart, find out what is wrong with it, and then put it back together again. He learns how to make Babbitt bearings using the shop molds. Even Big Jerr doesn't know how to do that.

He's often the runner who goes to Paul's Machine Shop and picks up reground crankshafts. He's fascinated by the machine tools and how they can be used to make and repair parts.

In the back end of the Ford shop is a special room that is closed off to everyone. He knows that what was going on in there is not part of the regular garage work as the lights are on late at night with work going on and no one is in there during the day. He becomes good friends with Jim Nielsen who only works at night and talks Jim into letting him go into the back room one evening while he's in there working all alone. What he sees amazes him.

There in the middle of the room sits a '34 Ford coupe with the body removed from the frame. The V8 flathead engine is mounted on the engine stand. He's never seen an engine built like this. It has aluminum heads and two carburetors where normally there was only one. The exhaust pipe is totally different as it is not one cast piece but three individual tubes on each side. The cylinder heads are not low compression cast iron but instead are high compression and made out of aluminum.

"This engine looks very special, Jim. Why is it made this way?"

"Jerr, you keep what you see here to yourself. I could be in big trouble if they knew I let you in here. This engine has double the horsepower of a factory engine and the chassis and brakes are very special as they are the late model hydraulic brakes, not the original mechanical ones. This car is being built for a bootlegger who has a still in the Smoky Mountains. This is the third one we have built for him. This car is faster than any other car on the road and can stop on a dime and give you nine cents change. If he's chased, he cannot be caught. He pays a lot of money to have these cars built in secret."

Wow! Jerr says to himself. He just wishes that he could build an engine like that.

Time To Fly The Nest

After returning from Charlotte Jerr starts to work full-time in the blacksmith shop, which is increasingly doing automotive modification and repair work. With the Ford Model T way down in price compared to other cars, it is becoming very popular with the hill folk. Big Jerr has a good business modifying them to do all sorts of things. By removing the rear wheel, he installs a belt drive and runs an electric generator or even a buzz saw. By the end of the summer, he's managed to build a new garage in front of the old forge shop and just uses the old shop for storage now as modern acetylene welding and stick-welding make it obsolete.

He tells Big Jerr all about the new things he learned at the Ford garage and even tells him about the bootlegger car.

"Now listen to me, Jerr, and you listen real good." He puts his face right in front of Jerr's face so there is no mistaking the stern look on it. "I know all about cars like that as there are guys in the hills that want them built and have asked me to build one. But I will not do it. It is a very risky business and not worth the extra money since trouble is seldom far away. You stay away from that. Your hear me?" With that said he goes back under a car to put in a new rear axle.

"Yes, I hear you and will keep my mouth shut." In his heart he knows that he must build engines like that but also knows that he cannot do it in Boone.

Little Jerr is not so little now. He's a full grown and handsome young man and quite in demand by the young ladies as a partner for square dancing. One of his buddies has a relative drive in all the way from California. Jerr gets to read a copy of the *L.A. Times* where in the want-ads he sees that The Douglas Aircraft Company is paying two dollars an hour for production machinists. Big Jerr can only afford to pay him seventy-five cents an hour to work in the garage.

He shows the advertisement to Big Jerr who says: "Listen, son, you're grown now and deserve to follow your own future. You take that job if you want it."

"But will you and Aunt Marge be OK if I don't work here anymore?"

"Don't worry about us; we will get along just fine. These old Model Ts and the new Model As and flathead V8s are more than enough work to keep us fed. Young Junior Roberts came by the other day and asked if I needed help. I can take him on as he's a good kid and should learn fast. Reminds me a little of you when you were younger."

In September, with everything settled between himself and his aunt and uncle, Little Jerr had taken the long bus and train ride to Los Angeles, watching out the window as the ripening fields of his home state gave way first to the desert, and then to the lush greens of southern California.

He'd landed a job as a lathe operator in the production area of the Douglas factory, but it isn't long before the bosses find out that he has a lot more talent and initiative than the run of the mill factory worker, and they offer him a twenty-five cent raise and a transfer to the prototype machine shop.

Jerr is really in his element now. The prototype shop is quite large with all kinds of the very best machine tools. He's put on a new Hardinge tool lathe—one of the best ever made. The quiet clean environment of the shop is such a contrast to the noisy production area with its screaming drills and rivet guns. He's now following blueprints to make some control rods for the coming advanced version of the Navy torpedo bomber.

Rex Takes Notice

The shop foreman and senior machinist is Rex Rutan. He's a large man but his smooth hands that have such a delicate touch on the controls of the machine tools betray an otherwise gruff exterior. Thirty years of practice on machining all types of materials make him an undisputable boss to the new men with less experience. If they will listen to him, they will learn. Jerr listens. Like any good foreman he maintains control of the work flow and quickly learns what the men in the shop are capable of doing. He soon learns that Jerr is a quick study. You only have to tell him once how to do something and he's able to get the job done right.

Jerr easily familiarizes himself with the Hardinge lathe and takes great interest in how to operate other machine tools. He's one of the few men in the shop that can read and understand the Machinists Handbook which is full of algebraic and trigonometric equations. He sometimes works out a solution to a problem that Rex is trying to solve. Rex sees a lot of potential in the young man.

Jerr is tightening some stock in the lathe's three jaw chuck when Rex interrupts him to meet a design engineer from upstairs in the aeronautical design department. The skinny guy is wearing a white lab coat over a gray shirt and blue tie. Clipped in the pocket of the shirt is a white plastic protector full of drafting pencils and a colored pen. Glancing through the mandatory steel rimmed safety glasses that are a requirement to enter the machine shop, he shakes Jerr's hand.

"Hello. I am John Wilhelm and I am the engineer responsible for the control rods that you are machining. I wanted to make sure that you are aware of the importance of the tight tolerance threads that we need for these rods. Rex tells me that the Hardinge lathe can hold these tolerances."

"Oh yes, it can do it. Here is a practice piece that Rex had me make. You can see that the thread gage fits it perfectly."

"That is nice work, Jerr. I can see that you really know what you are doing. I will stop being concerned about the quality of the machine work."

"John, may I ask you a personal question?"

"Sure."

"I want to learn how to do design work but do not know what education is required. What education do you have?"

"Well, Jerr, I graduated from Cal Tech in Pasadena with a bachelor's degree in aeronautical engineering."

"If I want to design an engine, what do I need to know?"

"Well, you have to know how to calculate static stress levels for non-moving parts and how to calculate dynamic forces acting on moving parts. You also have to know about fluid dynamics in order to understand how to make the engine powerful."

"Is that what they taught you?"

"Yes and some other stuff but those three courses are the most important."

Pasadena

Jerr gets permission to take a day off since he has worked a lot of overtime and some weekends. He takes the bus to Pasadena where he visits the Cal Tech campus. No one bothers him because he just looks like another student in a sea of students. With great excitement he sticks his head in some classrooms and watches like a fly on the wall the activity in an engineering lab. He had no idea that a place like this existed.

On a bulletin board he sees a notice that the new text books are now available at the bookstore. At the end of the hall in the engineering building he finds a campus map and locates the bookstore.

Oh man! Look at all those books piled on the tables covering most every subject you can think of. He zeros in on the engineering section and remembering John's explanation he searches for books on statics, dynamics and fluid mechanics. They are so expensive; one even costs twenty dollars. He cannot afford to buy them as he does not have that much cash. Then he notices a section with used books for sale at half price, and as luck will have it there are the books that he wants to buy. He has just enough cash to buy the three books with enough change left over to get home on the bus.

Back in his little Venice apartment he opens "Basic Principles of Mechanical Design" and starts reading. He now realizes how important Miss Johnson's tutoring was to him as the book is full of equations and with some difficulty he can understand them. He just talks out loud like he did with Miss Johnson. Somehow that helps him understand. Over the next few months he studies the other two text books. When he has questions he visits John Wilhelm at lunch time. John likes to help this kid that is so eager to learn.

During lunch break on Thursday he sits next to Tommy Thickstat on a bench in the break area outside the factory. It is a chance to enjoy some warm southern California sunshine under a couple of high palm trees.

"Can't wait until Friday and I can get out of here," says Tommy as he stands up and stretches.

"What's so special?" Jerr asks as he bites into his second bologna sandwich.

"Gonna' hitch up the trailer to my pickup, go over to Frank Brown's garage, pick up the belly tanker, and drive to the Bonneville Salt Flats where we want to set a speed record."

"What's a belly tanker? Jerr asks.

"Well, the unlimited salt flat speed racers like Frank buy war surplus fuel drop tanks that were used by fighter aircraft to extend their range. They're a perfect aerodynamic shape. Then they make a tube frame that carries the engine and drive line plus a little cockpit for the driver. I helped build the flathead Ford engine that runs it."

"Wow, that sounds exciting! I wish I could get in on a deal like that."

"Tell you what, Jerr, it's a 650 mile drive to Bonneville, and I sure could use a co-driver. Have to drive it straight through at night."

"Oh man, you can count me in!" Jerr is so excited he knocks over his bottle of orange soda.

Bonneville

Jerr and his new friend Tommy arrive at the Salt Flats at nine A.M. Frank and his young son Terry along with a kid named Tattersfield are waiting for them. They unload the belly tanker from the trailer in a hurry as they want to make a run before the air gets hot and robs them of power.

Jerr is fascinated at what he sees. The white Salt Flats are perfectly flat and perfectly white. There is absolutely no shade anywhere so they lay a tarp on the ground for their tools, spare parts and fuel cans. Jerr is just wearing a tee shirt but it's not long before he wishes he had long sleeves and a cowboy hat to protect himself from the brutal Nevada sun. Tommy gives him a pair of extra sunglasses from the truck or else he would have burned eyeballs.

"Hop in the truck," Tommy hollers. We're gonna' tow it to the starting line. There are six other cars in line ahead of them giving Jerr a chance to look around. Five of them are roadsters and one is a streamliner. They look and sound like nothing he has seen or heard before. He can feel their power and he tries to imagine how they became so different from the cars he sees on the street.

It was time for the belly tank to go. Such a sweet streamlined little machine built for nothing but speed. Jerr looks down the black stripe that is painted on the salt. It stretches out of sight. He can see the curvature of the earth in the distance.

"How far does it go?" Jerr asks.

"Course is seven miles. He has three miles to get up to speed and then gets his speed averaged over the fifth mile by very special time clocks. He has the rest of the course to get stopped."

They fire up the rear mounted flathead Ford V8 in the belly tanker. It barks to life with ear-splitting noise out of its three open exhaust stacks on each side of the tank. Frank Brown is ready to go as he pulls down the little Plexiglass bubble over his head.

Salt comes flying off his rear tires as he accelerates away from the starting line. There is no exhaust flame as the fuel is methyl alcohol which burns with an invisible flame. Soon he's just a dot on the horizon. In a few minutes word comes back over the loud speaker that he's timed at 180 mph through the traps. That'll be a record if he can get turned around in an hour and repeat the speed going the other direction.

Before the hour is up they have him turned around and launched on the return run. Then the loud speaker comes on and announces that the Brown Lakester aborted the run and is stopped off the course.

The belly tanker silently rolls into the makeshift pit on the end of a tow rope and is parked over the tarp spread on the ground. "What in hell happened?" Tommy asks Frank.

"Don't know. I was about to enter the time trap and the engine just lost power and started making a horrible noise. I shut it off and coasted off the course."

It doesn't take long for Tommy to remove the intake manifold from the top of the block. Peering down inside he immediately sees the problem. "The camshaft broke. A whole section is missing."

There's nothing to do now but load the belly tanker onto the trailer and head back to L.A. Tommy asks Jerr to drive as he's exhausted.

"Why did the camshaft break?" Jerr asks as sweat rolls down his back from the hot desert air blowing into the cab.

"There was probably too much stress on it from the high lift valves and stiff valve springs."

"Can you put in weaker valve springs?"

"Sure but then the valves will float at high rpm and skip over the lobes of the cam rather than follow them. It is really difficult to design the perfect camshaft. You improve one area of performance and it causes problems in another. We had the power but not the reliability. Back to the drawing board I guess."

The Inspiration

All the way back from the Salt Flats, Jerry is at the wheel of the pickup. Tommy is sound asleep with his head propped up against the window frame, exhausted from the excitement of the racing and unrelenting heat of the Nevada desert. The long drive is the perfect time for Jerry to let his creative mind work on the problem his friends encountered. He knows, based on his studies in dynamics that the camshaft failure was probably not the result of stiff valve springs, but perhaps due to resonance. Maybe Tommy would not be aware of this. "Back to the drawing board," Tommy had said. Yes, that was it! Jerr needed to try his own hand at designing the elusive but oh so vital camshaft. Then he'd be able to understand it statically and dynamically from the inside out and perhaps create a world record engine for the Brown Lakester.

He knows his innate feeling for metals and his ability as a machinist fed by his readings in technical books will all contribute to his vision of what he now has a burning desire to create. He knows, he just knows, that he can design and make a camshaft that will be the best ever made. Then he will build an engine that will power a car to new records.

After finally getting home, he's so consumed with the challenge that he can't sleep and barely feels like eating. So instead, he dips into his small "cookie jar" savings, and heads to the drafting store and buys a straight edge, a protractor, two dividers and a package of number two lead pencils. These plus some butcher paper and masking tape are all he's going to need. Then, at a nearby lumber yard he buys a smooth sheet of plywood and enough two by fours to make two high saw horses.

When he gets back to his one-room apartment in Venice, he makes a drafting table out of the homemade sawhorses and plywood, pushing it in front of the window and next to his bed. Knowing this is where he'll perch on a stool and spend most every free waking moment for the next week, he falls into an exhausted sleep.

Over the next week—just as he expected—he finds himself consumed with his evolving ideas about the camshaft. And with this surprising new skill, he finds that he can put what he imagines in his mind's eye down on the white butcher block paper.

He starts the design with just a simple circle and then closes his eyes and feels the flow of air through the four Stromberg 97 carburetors and into the Thickstun manifold. He feels it slam into the closed intake valve. Then with his pencil he draws the lobe of the camshaft to open the valve and let air push into the combustion chamber. Drawing the adjacent lobe, he opens the exhaust valve to let the burned gas out. It was Big Jerr and his harsh blacksmith lessons that taught him how to think about machines and metal, and he can almost feel the presence of his uncle beside him.

Now he tunes in to the engine's sound: the bellowing of the Blitzen Benz engine and its lazy power production anchors one end of his thoughts. At the other end is the scream of Frank Brown's flathead engine in the belly tanker as it flew over the Bonneville Salt

Flats close to a new speed record. He's going to unleash that power, plus more, to the road. There's no stopping him now. The cool Pacific breeze blowing through the window and over the drafting table acts as a radiator to cool his brain, and keeps him going without fatigue.

Suddenly it all comes together in Jerry's mind. The realization washes over him that the camshaft is the *heart* of the engine. To him, it really does become a pulsing heart, controlling valves designed to fly open and slam shut, and he knows all its secrets. He uses his mind to feel the rise and fall of the valves as they open and close. He knows intimately the precise fluid dynamics that will determine the flow of the fuel mixture. It is as if he can make himself a tiny particle that can travel through this engine controlled by the heart he's designing. He feels his way along through the carburetor and intake manifold to the top of the piston and then out the exhaust pipe, until he's sure the drawing is complete. Now comes the hard part—translating the vision on paper into the reality of motor-in-metal.

Titanium

Monday morning he walks into the Douglas factory thru the noisy assembly hanger with the sound of rivets being bucked and over to the machine shop where he's working on the control linkages. His mind is not on the Navy torpedo bomber that is taking shape as part of a special design project for the government. He's thinking about the metals that make up the experimental propeller of this very advanced prototype aircraft. It's the amazing properties of titanium that tickles his imagination. It's stronger than steel and much lighter. It'll take extreme temperature and will not corrode. This is the perfect material for his camshaft.

Since he and Tommy are now buddies, he asks Tommy about using titanium for the camshaft.

"No way, Jerr, you have two problems. First, it is hugely expensive, probably costs much more than you can afford and second, no one is quite sure how to machine a round billet, which is what you are going to have to do to make a camshaft out of it."

Hmm—Hmmm there has to be an answer Jerr thinks to himself. Just then Rex the shop foreman comes by.

"Rex, got a minute for a personal favor?"

Rex really likes Jerr as he always does excellent work, is able to solve problems on his own, and never complains about any assignment no matter how difficult.

"Oh sure, Jerr, what's on your mind?" Rex says as he pulls a Camel cigarette out of his brown machinist coveralls, lights it, and takes a big puff.

"Rex, would you be upset if I did a 'government job' on my own time?" Jerr knows that Rex would know as he does that a "government job" is a personal project done using company machines and often company material. It's frowned upon as it is forbidden by company rules but the blue collar guys carefully ignore the rule sometimes, and it is not a problem as long as the effort is not extensive and does not interfere with the schedule. A lot of really good ideas come out of these "government jobs," and in many ways they actually benefit the company.

"What you got in mind, Jerr?" Rex asks as he raises his voice to be heard over the screech of metal being turned on the big lathe behind them.

"Well, I want to experiment with learning how to machine titanium using a lathe and surface grinder."

"You'll certainly be on your own doing that as we can only cut it on the milling machine using tungsten carbide tools and even they have a problem. Who knows, you might discover something useful. Sure, go ahead. Just finish your regular jobs first. You can use anything that you find in the scrap bin." With that Rex ambles down the aisle with a blue cloud of cigarette smoke trialing behind him.

Jerr cannot wait until his shift is over and he can go digging in the scrap bin. It doesn't take him long to find a square bar whose dimensions can be made to work for the camshaft. He takes it over to his Hardinge tooling lathe, chucks it up, and starts experimenting with how to turn it into a round billet that will be the beginning shape for his camshaft.

Long Nights

Jerr is on his own on figuring out how to machine the titanium. But with his unique insight he's able to once again make the metal whisper to him and reveal its innermost secrets. He learns to go slow and to put a special shape on cutting tools that he makes out of tungsten carbide. Success does not come easy. When he has a failure he just sits back, eats a peanut butter sandwich, and thinks. Several loaves of bread and jars of peanut butter later, the camshaft finally takes shape.

It's actually Tommy that comes up with the novel idea that makes it possible to shape the lobes of the camshaft. He's friends with Ed Iskenderian of Isky cam fame. Since he used an Isky cam at Bonneville, he's treated with more than a little respect. Ed agrees to grind Jerr's profile on one of his chilled cast iron billets. With this as a pattern Jerr can then copy it onto the titanium billet.

Tommy stays over late this last night to watch Jerr do the final polish on the camshaft. It is a thing of real beauty that glistens like a jewel in the shop light. The Isky cast iron camshaft would break easily if you dropped it or used it like a baseball bat. You can drive nails with the feather light titanium camshaft. Jerr actually wets his pants a little he's so excited.

With the camshaft finished, he now turns his attention to the valve train and is able to make valves and valve retainers out of the same aircraft quality titanium. Because of its superior strength he decides to make the valve stems thinner and undercut the heads much greater than the stock valve. They are now both light, strong and will flow more air. More air means more horsepower. It all starts falling into place. With lighter free flowing valves, he can lift them faster and higher. Stronger valve springs would destroy the Isky cam, but for his cam it feels like a nice scratch on the back. The engine will be able to rev higher without valve float and that once again means more power.

With Tommy's help he secures a Mercury engine from a wrecking yard. It has a bigger crank than the Ford engine, and they make it even bigger by welding metal onto the throws and regrinding it. Now it is four and one-eight inches rather than the stock four. And while they are at it, they increase the bore to three and three-eights inches. They now have a 292 cubic inch engine rather than the stock 239 cubic inches of the Ford. All this means power, power, power!

It is as true for Jerr's engine as it was for the Blitzen Benz. When it comes to making power, there is no substitute for cubic inches. They now finish assembly of the engine in Tommy's garage by working late many nights and on the weekends. Now it sits ready to roar.

The '40 Ford Standard Coupe

Jerr is feeling a little foolish. He and Tommy have built a flathead Ford engine with a titanium camshaft that can challenge any race motor ever built, and they can't even start it. They have no car to put it in!

Even with his big pay check now that he's making two fifty an hour with overtime, he still has a problem saving money because he spends so much on books and engine parts. He and Tommy decide to cruise Figueroa Street in Tommy's '32 roadster to see if they can buy a used car to put the engine in. Tommy is all for getting a '32 Ford roadster as they are real cheap and have the great style that makes a hot rod a hot rod. But Jerr doesn't want one. There is no top on the car. He has seen guys come back soaked when they get caught in the rain.

The dealers all want to sell new cars or high priced used cars so they start cruising the gyp lots that have old cheap used cars. All they can find are old Packards, Cadillacs and Duesenbergs that were once used by movie stars, but they are of little value now except for scrap. Not finding anything, they start back to Venice a little discouraged. About a mile from the apartment Jerr says, "Whoa." Sitting in a driveway, way in the back, he sees a 1940 Ford Standard coupe. They hop out of the roadster and skip over to check it out. It's covered in a film of dirt and looks like it hasn't been washed or driven in a long time.

Just then an old man wearing a worn-out bath robe and slippers opens the back door and hollers: "What are you boys doing back there? This is private property."

Jerr responds, "Oh sorry, sir, we just got excited to see this old car back here and wonder if it is for sale."

"You got any money, son?"

"Yes, sir, I do," Jerr says and pats the pocket of his blue jeans. "Mind if we look at it?"

"No, go ahead, son, it's unlocked. I'll be out in a minute." The broken screen door bangs shut.

What Jerr discovers is that it's a 1940 Ford Standard coupe—the cheapest one made. There's no jump seat behind the driver's seat, just a package shelf connected to the big trunk. The puny little 60 horsepower engine does not allow the car to keep up with the fast L.A. traffic. Tommy ducks under the car and comes up smiling. It has the highly desirable Columbia two speed rear axle. In the front it has the tubular axle left over from the '37 Ford production run. Jerr wants this car. He knows how to make a hot rod out of it.

Jasper James, the owner, appears wearing bib overalls with nothing underneath them. Some chewing tobacco stains color his grizzled beard. "Five hundred dollars; take it or leave it."

Jerr and Tommy know better so they start bargaining with the old man. "Let's start it up and drive it to see if it runs OK."

"It don't start; battery is dead and gas is sour."

Jerr learned a lesson from his uncle on how to bargain. It is: Money talks and bullshit walks. He reaches in his pocket and takes out a roll of two hundred dollars in ten dollar bills and flashes it in front of the old man. He now owns a 1940 Ford.

Hot Rod

Back at the apartment driveway they rig up an engine hoist and pluck out the V8-60 engine and drop in the race motor, which fits in with very few problems. They rinse out the stale gas, put in some fresh gas, and fire up the engine for the first time. The engine is balky at first and billows a big cloud of blue smoke as the assembly grease burns out. Tommy adjusts the idle jets on the carbs and the engine settles into a smooth fast idle. It is pure music to their ears. Jerr is bursting with pride as he now knows his camshaft actually works. They let it run at fast idle for thirty minutes then turn it off and change the oil. With no mufflers or exhaust pipe, it makes a racket and the other tenants start to complain. Jerr rents a welding machine and with a trip to the parts store he can fabricate an exhaust system. With that done they are ready to try it on the street.

Jerr really does not know what to expect. Did he get the camshaft profile right? It does not take him but a minute to answer that question as he punches the throttle for the first time and the Ford takes off in wild acceleration. What happens next is not so good. Slamming on the brakes for a red light the car is barely able to stop.

A trip to the junk yard and fifty dollars later they have a set of big drum brakes off a wrecked Lincoln Zephyr. That cures the braking problem.

The next night they roam over to Wilshire Boulevard to see what action they can find. A lowered '50 Ford coupe challenges them at a stop light and they annihilate it. The '40 is FAST, FAST, FAST. On the next impromptu race, Jerr shifts the Columbia rear axle while under power and is greeted with a sickening noise as the differential case assembly cracks. The car limps back to Venice. He takes the differential apart and after his shift is over at Douglas, Jerr welds on a steel collar that makes it bullet proof.

Rose

Now that the '40 Ford is finished, Jerry wants to relax a little and enjoy it. While it is essentially a very fast race car, it can be driven normally if he just keeps his foot out of the firewall. This Saturday is going to be one of those beautiful sunny days that makes Los Angeles such a great place to live. In fact the population is growing so fast that they are planning to build special highways to accommodate all the traffic. Tommy had told him about the neat little seaside town of Pismo Beach that is a fun place to visit. He had gone there on a rod-run in his '32 roadster and had a great time.

He says that there's another rod-run going there this weekend and that Jerr should join up and have some fun. Jerr knows the hot rod boys have some really mean fast cars so he finagles some high octane aviation gas from the Douglas airfield pump and fills the tank on the '40. As he slides onto the cloth seats, he rolls down the windows and opens the cowl vent. The warm air feels just perfect as it blows through his tee shirt.

He joins up with the roadsters just north of the city and they head off along the coast highway toward Pismo Beach. The new engine is just so sweet. It does not purr like a kitten; it growls like a leashed tiger. If those roadsters want to get playful he can handle them. In a little over three hours they pull into Pismo and find an empty spot along the beach, take out some coolers and pop the caps on the beer bottles. This is such a great little place Jerr thinks; so far away from the bustle of L.A. He just lays back and soaks up the sun and listens to the waves gently lapping against the shore and watches the kids digging for clams.

Whenever the roadster boys go on a run they attract a lot of attention, particularly from the local girls. Today is no exception. It only takes about half an hour before some girls in an old woody Ford station wagon pull onto the beach. The giggly girls pile out and start inspecting the neat little roadsters with their hopped up flathead Ford engines that are still tinkling as they cool down. The guys are only too eager to show off the cars to them. One girl, a little older than the others and not so silly, saunters over to Jerr to look at his car.

"Hi, my name is Jerry Price. What's your name?"

"I'm Rose Donaldson," she replies with a smile on her face.

Jerr is thinking what a cute gal she's as he takes in her white tank top and short pants, which nicely fit her slim bottom.

"You live in Pismo Beach?" Jerr asks.

"No. I work as a secretary for the Town Clerk of Milford-Haven. It's a little town just north of here; kind of a jerk water place but I like it. We come down here to have fun and meet guys." She props herself against the fender of the '40. Jerr cannot help but notice that she's one very nice piece of work and seems so friendly. She's not like some of the Valley Girls in L.A. She seems much more homespun like the North Carolina girls that he dated before he left for the job at Douglas.

Just then one of the roadsters fires up with the sharp bark of a high compression flathead engine. The giggly girls are hopping in the cars. There are shouts about getting some burgers at the drive-in.

"Want a ride?" Jerr asks Rose.

"Sure, I've never been in a hot rod. Is this car fast?" She has no idea how fast it really is as the fastest she has ever been in a car is 70 mph in one of the local guy's Chevy six cylinder sedan. She thought that was a tremendous speed.

"Well, it can keep up with the traffic," Jerr says off-handedly. "Hop in."

Tommy pulls out ahead of the others and lays down some rubber as he takes off down the deserted stretch of the straight coast highway toward town.

"Wow, that fella' is fast. Can you catch him?" Rose asks.

"Hang on," Jerr shouts as he shifts the Columbia rear axle to low range, slams the column mounted gear shift into second gear, and pushes the accelerator pedal to the firewall. All the barrels of the three Stromberg 97 carburetors come open at once and they let out a deep moan as they suck in the air.

Rose is not ready for what happens next. She's pushed back into the seat as the Ford accelerates with a vicious snarl from the race tuned engine. The rpms rapidly climb to 6,000 and the snarl becomes a scream as the Ford rockets down the highway. It is only a few seconds before the speedometer pegs at one hundred but the speed keeps climbing. The Ford blows by Tommy like he's standing still.

Jerr lets off the gas as they enter the town and glances over at Rose. Her mouth is gaping open and she's as white as a sheet.

"Sorry, I didn't mean to scare you like that," Jerr says apologetically.

They park at the drive-in and Rose regains her composure.

Mrs. Jerry Price

The rod-run to Pismo Beach is only the start of several weekend trips for Jerr, but now the destination is Milford-Haven. He does these trips alone because he wants to be with Rose. She's living with her Aunt Marigold who has a small art gallery on Second Street. Jerry is polite but thinks the art looks like someone walked barefoot through spilled cans of paint. After a courteous hello they go to Pismo Beach and have fun surfing in the ocean. Surfing is a new sport for Jerr but he catches on quickly. At night he takes her back to Milford-Haven and they go to a little movie theater where they watch one of the very first Technicolor movies. After the movie they stop at the drugstore and get some Cokes then decide to go back to the beach.

They roam the beach in bare feet letting the waves lick at their feet. When they get back to the car, Rose turns her face to Jerr and he puts his strong arms around her and kisses her for the first time. As he opens the door and lays her across the seat of the coupe, Rose Donaldson starts her transformation to Mrs. Jerry Price.

They decide to have a quiet wedding in Las Vegas and except for Aunt Marigold, neither of them has family nearby. They find a new apartment in Santa Monica as the Venice apartment is too small for two. Fortunately Rose likes Jerry's hot rod buddies and they have fun with the guys and their dates. Jerr does tone his driving down though because Rose will not tolerate street racing. This becomes abundantly clear when one of the guys and his date get killed in an illegal race on the Pacific Coast Highway.

When Jerr comes home from work on Monday night, Rose is waiting for him with a very sad look on her face. She's holding a telegram.

"Here you better sit down and read this."

Your uncle Jerry died yesterday of a heart attack. (stop)
Please come home I need you (stop)

—Aunt Marge

Jerry buries his head in his hands and starts to cry. Rose puts her arms around him and comforts him. He tells Rose how Uncle Jerr and Aunt Marge took him in when his dad died and raised him as their own. He owes them everything and must go back and help.

Rose says she understands what he has to do and she wants him to leave for Boone immediately. She will wind up things in L.A. and take a train later to meet up with him. Jerry tells Rex on Tuesday that he has a family emergency and is forced to resign without notice. Rex is understanding and says the job if still open would be his if he wants to return.

"Jerr, there was something in the works that you do not know about. As you are well aware, I work very closely with engineering on the fabrication that we do in the shop." Rex continues, "I told the chief engineer about how you designed and fabricated a titanium camshaft and made it work in an engine. He was very impressed and said that if you wanted to sign an employment agreement he would see that The Douglas Aircraft Company gives you a scholarship to Cal Tech where you can take courses to become an aeronautical engineer."

"The hell you say? Wow, what an opportunity!" Jerr's face is beaming. "Me—an engineer?" With slumping shoulders he looks Rex in the eye. "Rex, I just cannot stay in L.A. I have an obligation back home that is just too big and I must go there."

With a fond glance and final inspection of his beloved Hardinge lathe, Jerry leaves The Douglas Aircraft Company never to return.

Price's Garage

With Rose's help Jerry puts his clothes in the spacious trunk of the Ford and heads out right away for Boone, North Carolina. It is going to be a grueling 2,400 mile trip across the desert and the open spaces of the Southwest. He drives at a steady seventy mph, which is easy on the engine as he keeps the Columbia in the overdrive range to conserve gas. He makes it to Albuquerque via Route 66 arriving late at night, pulls off onto a side road and sleeps in the car.

It's Route 66 all the way to Oklahoma City. From there he breaks off Route 66 and heads for Little Rock, Arkansas. To save a few dollars he buys some gas from a local unbranded station—a big mistake. It is low octane gas that causes his engine to detonate and rattle like a baby's toy. He slows way down and burns off the bad gas to save the engine. With good gas in the tank, he makes it into Little Rock very late. His arms are dead tired and his eyes sting, and his right foot is cramping from pressing on the gas pedal. Stopping at a cheap tourist cabin, he collapses into a worn-out, lumpy mattress and is dead to the world.

Refreshed and with no further problems, he finally makes it through the mountains and into Boone and the waiting arms of

Aunt Marge. Marge looks older now; her hair has turned grey. They visit Big Jerr's grave still covered with beautiful mountain flowers.

Jerr is now aware that he has a new responsibility and that it is up to him to not only care for Rose but also Marge. Maybe move to Charlotte or Raleigh and get a job in a machine shop? But then he looks around some more. The old garage has been expanded and there is a new sign over it that spells out: PRICE'S GARAGE. Now he thinks why not just stay here and pick up where Big Jerr left off? There is the house, the garage and the old blacksmith shop that is now part of a junkyard for old cars and farm machinery. He sends for Rose who makes the long trip by train and Greyhound bus. It takes her a couple days to get to Charlotte where Jerr picks her up for the final leg to Boone.

Junior Roberts

It's two days after Jerr gets to Boone that Junior Roberts drops by after school is out. He wants to know if he can still keep working at the garage. Jerr knows he will need some help. This quiet fourteen-year-old kid has some muscle on him and Big Jerr had said that he was a good worker and came from a good family. He puts Junior to work after school and weekends pumping gas and changing oil.

One afternoon while Jerr is on a creeper putting new rod bearings in a Model A Ford, he hears a commotion outside. It's old Mr. Cahn threatening Junior because he hit his bully of a son at school. Jerr slides out from under the car to see what is going on and sees that old man Cahn has Junior by the collar and is about to punch him.

"Hold on there!" Jerr shouts as he grabs a tire iron off the bench. "You leave that kid alone or you will have to deal with me. Get the hell off my property."

Furious, Mr. Cahn leaves but Jerr thinks the confrontation is sure to have future consequences. Mean hill folk like him can be very nasty and have long memories. But one thing Jerr learns is that Junior will not take guff from anyone. He likes that about him.

It hadn't taken long for word to spread in the little town of Milford-Haven that Aunt Marigold's niece Rose had gotten herself hitched to a man with a fast car. That's how it was in small towns—everyone knows everyone else's business. Jerr had to remember that Boone, unlike Los Angeles, would be just the same. He learns from Frank Stearns who owns the grocery store that Pa Roberts has been buying 100 pound bags of sugar. That can mean only one thing. He's running a still to make illegal white lightening.

Junior is now sixteen and has been working at the garage part-time for several years. They really like each other a lot. Junior has learned to drive and loves it. He can't wait to deliver a car to a customer. He even drives Jerr's Model A truck to Charlotte to pick up parts. He's a very fast driver but keeps a car under control. Jerr thinks he may have a special driving talent.

Jerr has been watching Junior and senses that the lad is fighting some sort of problem. Usually he's totally focused and enthusiastic about what he's doing, but lately he's distracted and making mistakes. This morning he had forgotten to take the gas pump nozzle out of Doc Franklin's Model A and gas poured out over the cowl with fumes spilling into the garage. Immediately signaling danger to Jerr, he grabs the radiator water can with the goose neck spout and pours water over the cowl of the Model A before the fumes can get thick enough to ignite on the tinkling hot exhaust manifold. Junior apologizes to Doc and uses a clean shop rag to wipe up the water. He peers into the open gas tank to be sure that there is no water leaking into it and with his powerful plow strengthened forearms quickly twists the gas cap shut.

The white clouds that covered the sun in the morning have rolled past and with a big blue sky the heat of the day has arrived. Rose picks up the clear glass gallon jar of sun tea that she has brewing on the window ledge of the kitchen and dumps in a cup full of sugar to make the "Sweet Tea" that is so popular with the locals during the hot Appalachian summer.

The old oak tree in front of the unused blacksmith shed makes for some much welcome shade. Jerr often wonders if Daniel Boone himself had sat under that tree. Some seats from a wrecked Model T make for a good resting place after sweeping dozens and dozens of old fallen acorns off of them.

"Junior, stop what you are doing and come sit a spell." Junior ambles over and sits beside Jerr. Using a grease-stained shop rag that was once a pair of Jerr's long johns, they take turns wiping the sweat off their faces.

Rose comes outside and hands each a big glass of the tea that she has cooled with ice chipped off the frozen block that keeps food in the old ice box cool. Jerr has been saving up to buy a new electric refrigerator so they do not have to depend on the ice man coming around once a week.

Following some big gulps of the sweet tea, they stretch out their tired legs. Jerr now senses that Junior is relaxed and ready to listen to what he has to say. "Junior, I think you better tell me what your dad is doing. You know that he's headed for trouble."

At first, Junior tries to be evasive, but he has no gift of guile so he breaks down and tells Jerr about his family's plight. They are very poor and his ma is very sick. And the only way they can make money is to sell shine to Jack Mayberry, the John Deere salesman, who has a distributor in Bristol. He goes on to tell Jerr that he and his dad know who the distributor is in Bristol and they plan to deliver directly to him and cut out Jack.

Junior says that they bought the widow Webb's '40 Ford Standard coupe and he's going to start making deliveries. Jerr's hair just about stands on end from hearing this news. This kid is headed for big trouble. He will either get caught by the government agents or hijacked by another bootlegger. He knows that car with the sixty horsepower engine because he has worked on it. On the surface it is identical to his hot rod but it will barely make it over the mountain if it is loaded with Mason jars full of shine. The old blacksmith shed is no longer used so Junior doesn't know about Jerr's hot rod Ford coupe locked up inside.

"Junior, it is against my better judgment but I am going to help you. Your car is no *shine* car. I know that you and your pa are desperate, but you are headed for very big trouble and I don't want that for you. You bring that car in next week and I will take care of it. It is going to cost you and your pa but you can pay me as you get paid." Junior cannot wait to get home and tell his pa. He jumps on his Schwinn bicycle and pedals like mad toward the farm.

The Big Switch

Just as Jerr figured, Junior gets in big trouble when he tries to make a premature run in the unmodified Webb coupe and gets chased by federal agents. The next afternoon he delivers the car to Jerr to modify. Jerr tells Junior it will take just two weeks but that is a big lie. It took him many months to build his hot rod. What he's going to do is take his hot rod and beef up the suspension to handle a load of shine and sell it to Junior. He will take Junior's car to Charlotte and put it in trade for a new pickup for the garage. Junior will never be the wiser. He just hopes that Junior can avoid serious trouble as illegal whiskey just draws trouble like a moth to a flame.

Junior picks up the hot rod thinking it is widow Webb's car completely modified by Jerr. He starts his regular runs to Bristol and he and his pa are making a mattress full of money. Jerr's notion is correct. It turns out that Junior is a fantastic driver—far superior to the federal agents and other bootleggers. The race-tuned flathead '40 Ford with its titanium camshaft engine can outrun anything on the road.

It isn't long before Jerr and Junior begin to cook up a new idea. Why not build a stock car racer together and have Junior race it?

They pull a junked '36 Ford coupe out of the boneyard and build a stock car racer and take it to the North Wilkesboro race track where Junior wins most all the races that he enters. Needless to say it has one of Jerr's special engines slinging it out of the curves and sending it like greased lightning down the short straight stretches.

But also his fear comes true. The sad thing is winning at the track still isn't enough for Junior. He keeps running shine for his pa. Junior gets caught when a squealer fingers him and he spends two years in prison. There is no chance for him to get a regular job now that he has a prison record.

Older now and much more mature after his two-year prison experience, he still has a burning desire to drive and race. Jerr talks it over with Rose and a decision is made to build and sponsor a race car for Junior.

The Price-Roberts race team begins to make history. They are a great success in the newly formed NASCAR race circuit. They win and win big. This attracts sponsors as television goes nationwide. They are forced to leave Boone behind to set up a major racing operation in Charlotte. Rose, always ready for a new adventure with her husband, packs up their modest house in Boone and gets a beautiful big new home in Charlotte. Of course, she has to do something about filling up all those extra bedrooms, so she starts by presenting Jerr with a fine baby boy.

Vengeance

Stanley Cahn, the class bully that Junior punched out in grade school, hasn't learned much about ethics or the law during all this time. He's become a bootlegger, and he's a very successful one.

His success is due partly to his good driving, but there's more to the story. He becomes a distributor too, one with an unscrupulous and vicious partner—his own dad, who simply uses his twelve gauge shotgun to destroy all competition. Stanley and his dad make so much money that they can now afford to have a race team just like Jerry and Junior. They start showing up at the track, intending to give the Price-Roberts race team a run for its money. What they don't have is Junior's extraordinary skill as a driver and Jerry's extraordinary skill as a designer and builder.

Whenever they are in the same race, it is Junior who comes in first with Stanley second. Stanley and his old bastard of a dad are gradually eaten up inside with extreme jealousy. "Look, son," the resentful dad says, "you have got to do something about Junior. He's keeping us out of the big money every time we race."

"Next race I *will* take care of him. I owe him one from way back and it will be my pleasure to collect." Stanly spits it out with clenched teeth as he straps on his race helmet and stuffs his legs through the window of his Dodge stock car.

Junior is already on the Charlotte race track in his Boss 429 Ford Torino taking a warm-up lap. Both cars are extremely fast and capable of hitting close to 200 mph on the back straight. Junior starts from the pole position and leads the race. After 45 laps he has to stop for gas and tires. This allows Stanley to catch up with him. At the entrance to turn three on the high bank Stanley is on Junior's bumper as Junior is still coming up to speed. He sees his chance to wreck him now as all he has to do is touch the left side of his bumper. That'll send him into a skid and into the wall and wreck his car and—hopefully—kill him.

Junior has seen Stanley's tricks before when he wrecked other cars and is ready for him. He ducks down low taking the down force air pressure off Stanley's Dodge. This upsets his steering just as he's trying to bump Junior. It throws *him* rather than Junior into a high speed skid and into the wall followed by a rollover slide to the infield. His Dodge is wrecked but he walks away. Junior once again beats the bully.

Old man Cahn is furious at the unexpected outcome of their plan. He chews Stanley up one side and down the other. "OK so Junior has your number. Well, there's more than one way to skin this cat."

The next race is at one of the older tracks that does not have a separate lane with a guard rail to protect the pit crews from the race cars on the track. Old man Cahn tells Stanley to get his ass in the trailer as he has some instructions for him. When Stanley comes out he has a real mean look on his face. Old man Cahn spits some tobacco juice and heads for the track rail.

It is a 200 lap race. On lap 147 Jerry crosses the track guard rail and onto the track to signal Junior to come in for another pit stop. Stanley comes screaming out of turn four seemingly totally out of control. He broad slides the Dodge to scrape the rail at just the spot where Jerry is standing. Jerry is knocked over the rail.

Everyone watching the race is horrified, hardly able to believe what they've seen. Could the great race car builder Jerry Price have survived the impact of his competitor's car? Fortunately Jerry saw the skidding Dodge with only an instant to spare and had started to leap over the rail just as he got struck. He had a broken leg but luckily no other serious injuries.

They called it a racing accident but this was no accident. It was a vicious murder attempt and all the other teams know it. At the Daytona race Stanley is bumped by two cars acting together and flies over the turn four wall at 190 miles per hour with such force that the engine is ripped out of the car and sent flying into a parking lot. The Dodge hits nose first and explodes in flame. Stanley does not make it out. Later that month a shotgun blast by an old bootlegger ended his dad's life. Evil to him who lives an evil life.

Everything Changes

Rose catches up with Jerry in the hospital emergency room and watches while they put a cast on his leg. Once up in the private hospital room, she knows that it is time to talk to him about what has been on her mind for some time.

"Jerry, I know how much you love racing and how racing has made it possible for us to have a really nice home and give Jerry Junior advantages that we never had. But I think we have to face a new reality. This is a young man's game and you are middle-aged now. We need to think about our future. You cannot go on racing forever." With Jerry in pain Rose knows what she's saying might upset him but it needs to be said as only a loving wife can say it.

"You have been so tied up with NASCAR and racing that you really don't know how successful our son has been with the dealership. He has worked hard and worked smart and has made Priceland Ford the number two Ford dealer in Charlotte. I think it's time we recognized his hard work, quit racing and help him grow the dealership to number one. What do you think, hon?"

"Oh, Rose, bless your heart. I guess I have been too absorbed with racing to be of help to you and Jerr Junior. I have an idea." Jerry's leg cast is starting to itch and it is painful. He takes a couple of aspirin and shifts his weight. "This may sound a little strange but I think we can make it work. Young Jerr really likes and understands how a race team operates and has been doing a great job with the pit crew on race days. I think he's capable of running the team, particularly if I can back him up. Junior Roberts is still a competitive driver but he also is coming to the end of his career so now is a good time to make changes. I think he will stay on to help our boy find a new winning driver. What do think, Rose?"

Yes, I love the idea. Our boy is not a driver but he does love racing and knows how to be a good manager. I think that we can make this work. I do so love you, Jerry."

Old Man Price

And so it came to pass. Jerry Junior takes over the team and dad becomes the full-time manager of Priceland Ford and makes it not only the number one dealership in Charlotte but in the entire southeast. As a side business he opens a race shop called "Price and Son Performance Engines." It becomes the go-to shop for race teams that want a winning Ford engine.

Next to the engine shop is a small garage with no sign on it. To all eyes it is just a storage unit. Inside you can find a Ford Galaxy sedan with a beefed up suspension and SOHC 427 race motor. No way is this a NASCAR track car. No rules apply to this car. It is so fast and handles so amazingly at high speeds that even a race car cannot catch it. It is owned by a friend of Jerr's in the growing town of Boone. Enough said—just stay out of there.

In Centennial, Colorado, there is an old '40 Ford Standard coupe that has an unknown history. It is a very fast car and still has an old flathead engine, except the Ford cylinder heads have been replaced with high performance Baron heads. It is often challenged to an impromptu street race by a modern car. The modern car always loses. Upon inspection of the engine it is discovered that it has a titanium camshaft. Who on earth would make something like that?

Return soon to . . .
Charles S. Clark's Hot Rod Adventures!

Here's an excerpt from
The Bootlegger '40 Ford

Novel One in the exciting
Hot Rod Adventures

Excerpt from Part 1:
White Lighning:
The Strange Odyssey of a $500 Car

Part 1:
White Lightning
The Strange Odyssey of a $500 Car

70

CHAPTER ONE

In the Beginning

The hills of North Carolina were a tough place to make a living. The earth was good in the bottom land but rapidly turned to hard scrabble as it rose up to form the scraggy hills of the Appalachian mountains. The ice-age glaciers clawed out the ground like a set of giant fingers and left a pile of rocks, the biggest of which formed the Smoky Mountains. The farmers who settled on this marginal land were a proud lot, and by force of will plus a lot of sweat and muscle, wrestled a living from this hard land. It was into one such proud, but poor, farm family that Junior Roberts was born in 1936, the only child of Seth and Mary. From the time he left his mother's nipple he was given to understand that he had a place and purpose in the family. As a young child he walked behind his father as he plowed the corn field with a mule. They may have been poor in material goods but because they were intelligent and diligent farmers, they ate well from their own crops and livestock. When the hormones hit, Junior turned into a strapping young man with legs and shoulders made powerful by pushing a plow behind a stubborn mule.

Junior's education was basic but adequate in the one room schoolhouse. All the kids were well mannered or got whipped when they got home. Discipline was not only expected, it was demanded. The families knew only too well that their children's future depended on education and they took it very seriously.

But kids will be kids and they had to test the social order. Junior, to observe him, seemed like a sluggish kid with sleepy eyes hidden under big bushy lashes. He didn't say much and was well liked by the other kids with the exception of Stanley Cahn, the class bully. Stanley saw Junior as a threat to his control of the rest of the school kids, since Junior simply ignored Stanley and his domineering behavior. One afternoon, Stanley set out after Junior and provoked him in the hopes of starting a fight.

Junior just ignored him as usual, with his sleepy eyes barely moving to either side. Stanley couldn't handle such indifference so he wound up to deliver a sucker punch to Junior's nose. With lightning reaction, Junior ducked under Stanley's moving arm and his big fist, driven by forearms made powerful from pushing the plow, buried itself into Stanley's belly. Stanley doubled up and collapsed with a moan and Junior just strode away without changing his sleepy expression. Stanley's attitude changed; Junior was the boss now.

Junior's mother was quite ill. It was not an uncommon event in those days but the effects were devastating. It started out as a cold or the flu but quickly progressed to something much more serious. The fever came in waves and each successive wave caused his mother to lose more of her strength. The doctor called it undulant fever and said it was probably due to some bad milk that she drank. Pasteurization of milk, which killed the Brucella bacteria, was not practiced in the small hill country dairies. When it had run its course his mother changed from a vibrant buxom woman who commanded the household, to a frail middle-aged lady who had to conserve what little strength she had, to see to the most essential chores. Junior's father had a hard time coming to grips with the new reality of their household. He became irritable and cranky and bitter at the circumstance. He truly loved his wife and could not accept what had happened to her.

His mother's failing health forced Junior to accept responsibility that really belonged on the shoulders of a mature man. But Junior did not flinch. He became more involved with his father in running the farm and securing a living for the family. He also learned the hard reality of marginal farming in North Carolina. Without a cash crop like tobacco to sell, the family could barely survive.

An Ulterior Motive

It was not chance or fate that brought the tractor salesman, Jack Maybary, to the Roberts' door, but a carefully conceived sinister marketing strategy hidden behind the veil of a legitimate business enterprise. Jack was a farm boy from Iowa and knew the tractor business. He used to work in a John Deere dealership in Mason City, Iowa, where he quickly discovered that selling a tractor was a whole lot easier than plowing with one, or fixing it when it broke. So he learned how to sell and, after a struggling start, became very good at it. So good that he was given a sales territory that covered the western hills of North Carolina down to Bristol, Tennessee, and some of Southwest Virginia. It didn't take Jack very long to discover that the territory was as barren as the small farms located in it. With some exceptions, everyone wanted a tractor to replace the damned old mules, but few could afford one. Jack was about to give up when he made a discovery that set the course for both his and Junior's future.

What Jack discovered was that there were a lot of thirsty young soldiers trying to live off Army pay. They wanted to drink the bonded whiskey sold in the liquor store but it was too expensive, and, in the dry counties, it was unavailable, because it was illegal to sell. What made the bonded whiskey so expensive was the tax placed on it by the federal government. "Bonded" meant that the tax had been paid and the whiskey was legal to sell in those counties where the law allowed it. This resulted in the manufacture of illegal whiskey made out of fermented corn.

Some called it "corn whiskey" and others called it "white lightning" because of its clear color and high alcohol content. Another common name was "moonshine" or just "shine" since it was often made at night in a clandestine still. One-hundred proof was a low end value for this home brewed inebriant.

Of course it was made without the quality control of the big distilleries. Some of it was smooth and as tasty as anything Seagrams could turn out. Then there was the rotgut loaded with aldehydes and other poisonous byproducts of careless distillation. All of it found a ready market, and a good bootlegger could make a small fortune selling it. Of course the feds did not take kindly to the loss of revenue and the local sheriffs had to enforce the law on behalf of the tee-totaler electorate. The jails had a wide open one-way door for those unfortunate enough to get caught making or selling the illegal whiskey. The idea was to be smart and careful. Jack was both.

Jack knew that all the hill people could make white lightening. It was a part of the culture. Most of them just made enough for their own consumption and sociability with their friends. They couldn't give a tinker's dam for the federal government and its sin tax on alcohol. It was his plan to visit the farms as a tractor salesman and literally sniff out those who could make good shine and seduce them into becoming his supplier.

The Devil's Bargain

"Good afternoon mister Roberts. Hot day for this time of year." said Jack in his most cheerful salesman voice. "I'm Jack Maybary of the John Deere company and I am stopping at farms in the valley to introduce myself and acquaint you with the fine tractors I sell."

"Might as well have saved yourself the trip, Mr. Maybary. John Deere is a fine tractor but my old mule is all I can afford," sighed Mr. Roberts.

"Well, it's my job to make the unaffordable, affordable to honest hardworking men like yourself who could really benefit from a great piece of machinery. Like they say you've got to spend money to make money. Don't you agree?"

"Hell yes I agree, but first you have to have the money to spend."

"OK, now we are getting somewhere. You agree you need the tractor but the problem is getting the where-with-all to pay for it." Jack opined in a very sincere manner. "If I can show you how to pay for a tractor, will you buy it from me?" Jack was going for a fast close.

"Hold on just a moment young fella. Not so fast. You've got some explaining to do. How does a hill farmer like me with a sick wife and a young boy to care for get money for a fancy tractor?"

"Sorry to hear about your wife, Mr. Roberts, and that is certainly a fine looking young man you have for a son. I would really like to help you if we could spend a few minutes to explore your situation," Jack said with a smile in his voice.

"May as well spend some time jawing with you. Nothing else seems to be working for me," Mr. Roberts said in a low voice reflecting his inner discouragement.

"Mr. Roberts, you sound like a man who needs a little pepping up and I'm about to fade out from the exertion of wandering around these hills. You wouldn't have a little pick-me-up around would you?" The Devil was at work now.

"Step in the barn and I'll see if there's any squeezins left in the jug." With that Mr. Roberts took a couple of tin cups off a nail and headed for a corner of the barn. "Yup, looks like the old jug hasn't dried up yet." He poured a couple of stiff jolts into the cups. "Well, Mr. Maybary, here's to you and your tractor." He swallowed the contents in one gulp, pursed his lips and shook his head.

"Here's to you, your fine family and a prosperous future, Mr. Roberts." Jack swallowed the shine down "neat." His reaction was instantaneous. This was good stuff! No burning, just a smooth warming of his esophagus and stomach. "Mr. Roberts, that is some of the finest whiskey it has ever been my privilege to drink. Mind if I ask where you got it?"

"Didn't get it anywhere. Made it myself, Mr. Maybary, just like my pappy and his pappy before him," Mr. Roberts intoned with pride in his voice. The whiskey was starting to do its job on his brain.

"Look, just call me Jack. I'm a farm boy just like your son and while I want respect like any man, I also like to make friends." Jack was on a roll.

"Fair nuf Jack, call me Seth and that's Junior over there," Seth said as mellow glow started to come over him.

"Junior, pleased to meet you. It's a pleasure to shake hands with such a fine young man." He reached in Junior's direction. He was not prepared for the vice that griped his fingers. Junior didn't know his own strength. Jack tried not to wince.

"Seth, I just had a thought that I think I need to share with you. My travels take me all over this area and I know for a fact that there are honest, god-fearing people that will pay good money for a quality refreshment like this."

"Hold on now Jack, I may be a poor dumb farmer but I know that selling unbonded whiskey is illegal," said Seth as he stiffened his posture.

"Hold on yourself Seth. Who said anything about you selling illegal whiskey? Besides, who made it illegal and why? It was those worthless politicians up in Washington, that's who. They did it to squeeze another nickel out of the working man. That's why!" Jack was into it now. He had his spiel well rehearsed and the shine just made it come out that much better. "If a working man makes a quality product that another working man wants to enjoy, why should it be any of the government's business?" He held out his cup and Seth filled up both of their cups.

"Well I can't disagree with your logic, but I'm not going to jail so another man can have a good drink!"

"Couldn't agree with you more, Seth. You think I want to go to the pokey? Not on your life. But I tell you what, I don't turn my back on making a little extra money if the opportunity is right and, I think if we tried just a little, we could make the right thing happen. I don't have anyone doing me favors when it comes to making a living. Do you?" Jack turned his devil eye towards Seth.

"Start explaining," said Seth as the alcohol started to take hold of his judgment.

"Suppose you were to put up about ten quarts of that fine brew in some Mason jars. And suppose when the milk truck came around, the driver moseyed innocent-like into the barn and took those jars out with the milk cans. Then suppose I came around and put a fifty-dollar bill in your hand? Tell me who sold what to whom if anyone asks, and who is going to ask? You had a sneak thief take advantage of you. The fifty dollars is between you and me, not you and the milkman. Everyone makes a profit and no one gets hurt. Now what's wrong with that Seth?" Jack had his fish hooked right to the guts. He now had his ninth supplier.

After shaking hands to seal the deal, Jack casually gave Seth a twenty-dollar bill for "supplies" and headed for his car. Jack was a little guy and the white lightening was about to overpower him. With a pleading look he turned to Seth and said, "You don't suppose you could spare Junior to drive me back to town. I just don't feel up to it myself."

Seth cracked a big smile at the hot-shot salesman who couldn't hold his licker. "Sure. Go ahead Junior, take the man back to town. You can ride back with the doc in the morning when he comes out to see ma."

CHAPTER TWO

Junior Makes a Discovery

Up to this moment Junior had been his passive, observant self. But now his eyes came alive with the thought of driving the salesman's new Oldsmobile sitting in the driveway. It was a 1950 Holiday hardtop coupe with the Rocket 88 engine. He had never seen a more desirable car. Junior's only driving experience was in Model A Fords that hung around the old farms as last vestiges of the great depression. He had never driven a modern car. The fact that he was only fourteen-years-old didn't phase anyone. Hill kids did what they could when they could. The law just looked the other way as there was no need to kick up a fuss.

Jack gave Junior cursory operating instructions on the Olds and then promptly conked out as Junior rolled out of the driveway. With a quick wave to his pa, Junior headed down the narrow country road. The Olds was a total revelation to Junior. The old Model A's just sputtered and growled as they banged along the country roads. The Olds just glided as if on a cloud. The powerful V8 engine just burbled as speed started to build. Unknown even to himself, Junior had a gift for driving. His senses worked in perfect coordination. The motion of the car blended into his mind and became an instinctual part of his being. His big powerful shoulders and arms were connected by fast firing nerves to his eyes and inner ear. The mighty Olds responded as part of his body, gracefully sweeping from curve to curve. By the time he reached the state road, Junior and the car had fused into one machine, half human and half metal.

The road to Bristol had very little traffic on it as it wound its tortuous way through the hills and hollows. It wasn't long before Junior and the Olds were in full flight. On the straights he would push up to ninety miles an hour and then smoothly brake into the curves as he let the car drift across the apex in one coordinated movement. If Jack had been awake he would have been aghast at what this child was doing with his new car. As it was, he snored the miles away until the outskirts of Bristol. Junior gently jarred him awake and got directions to his boarding house. Jack looked at his watch and shook it.

"Anything wrong?" Junior asked.

"No, its just running way slow. It says it's less than an hour since we left your place and it takes two hours to get here. I'll have it checked tomorrow." Jack put Junior up in a spare room. He got up early in the morning and went over to doc's office so he could go on rounds with him as he worked his way toward home and his anxious ma and pa.

Business is Good

Mister Roberts was true to his word and Jack kept his end of the bargain. Once a week the milk man would pick up ten Mason jars and twice a month Jack would come round with one-hundred dollars in ten dollar bills in a plain envelope. The pact had been made with the Devil and he wasn't about to ease up. Soon the milkman was picking up twenty jars instead of ten and the envelope from Jack got twice as fat. The economic situation for the Roberts' family changed drastically. Now ma Roberts got special medical attention and Pa got his new John Deere tractor. Junior just kept on growing and watching through those sleepy eyes. At age sixteen he finished school and started helping his pa full-time. He was no fool. He knew that what his pa was doing was illegal, but he also knew that his ma was getting stronger with the extra medical attention. His first and only loyalty was to his family and he was going to do his part, legal or not.

Pa Roberts was not an original thinker. He just did a job as it presented itself. But Junior was cut from his mother's cloth and like her, he silently questioned everything around him. Mostly he had questions about Jack and the money that was being made selling the shine that he and his father so carefully distilled and bottled. One day when he took his ma to Bristol for an overnight checkup at the clinic, he did a little snooping around. What he discovered rapidly changed his life from that of an innocent lad to one of a sharp entrepreneur.

At night without being seen he caught Jack talking to his distributor who, much to the shock of Junior's innocent mind, turned out to be the rector of the Episcopal church. When Junior peeked through the high window in the big carriage house behind the parsonage he could make out a large covered pile of what he knew to be Mason jars. He boldly crept closer to the front of the house where he could hear Jack and the parson talking. Jack was explaining that his costs were going up and that the next load was going to cost $15 dollars a jar and the good hill stuff would cost twenty. Junior immediately sensed that "the good hill stuff" came from their farm.

So that was it. Jack paid his pa five bucks and collected twenty from the parson. Now that he knew who was buying the stuff why did they need Jack? They could triple or quadruple their income by selling direct to the parson. Junior's young mind was in high gear now. He would have a talk with his pa.

"Pa, it just ain't right. Here we break our back lugging stuff up to the hollow so we can still up some licker and this guy Jack just tells a truck driver to pick it up and take it to the parson. Then he picks up a fat envelope from the parson and hands us a skinny one. Now that ain't right and we are stupid for putting up with it."

"Who you calling stupid son?" his pa snapped.

"Oh come on Pa, I'm not saying you are stupid. I am saying the situation is stupid and we need to do something about it," Junior replied in a calm tone. He had a natural instinct for diplomacy.

His pa calmed down and they started talking logically about the situation. Who would contact the parson to set up the deal and how would they transport the shine to Bristol?

After some discussion they agreed upon a plan. Mr. Roberts would meet with the parson. As an adult he would have more credibility than Junior. If they lost the parson, there could be no deal, so the approach would have to be very cautious. Handling Jack would be easy. They would just tell him they had made all the money they needed and were getting out of the moonshine business. Pa Roberts would thank him kindly for all his help and leave him smiling.

They figured that Jack was not the only one who could set up a deal. Junior said he would come up with a way to get the shine to Bristol. He already had a plan in mind.

The next week when it came time for ma to go in for another checkup, it was pa who took her in their new Chevrolet sedan. While ma was at the clinic pa excused himself to attend to some other business. He drove over to the parsonage where he had already set an appointment with the parson. The parson assumed they were going to talk about some religious need such as a funeral or a wedding. He was taken completely by surprise when Mr. Roberts asked him if he knew Jack Maybary. Without changing his expression the parson pretended to think and then opined; "Isn't he the drummer that sells John Deere tractors?"

"That's the man," Pa said. "I also happen to know that he sells something else."

"Oh, what's that?" said the parson in a non-committal voice trying to cover up his nervousness.

"Now don't get excited," said pa in a calm voice. "I'm not here to make trouble. I'm here to make you an excellent business deal. That good shine that you buy from Jack comes from my farm. My boy and I are the only people on God's green earth that knows he sells it to you and now you know that I make it. You see we both have reasons to keep our mouths shut." The red flush started to recede from the parson's face.

"What sort of business deal do you have in mind, Mr. Roberts?"

The conversation didn't last long as the deal was quite simple. Mr. Roberts would keep the old price and deliver the shine directly to the parson's carriage house. The parson would pay on delivery. After each delivery a schedule would be set up for the next delivery. The parson would wean Jack down on the orders he gave him and replace the lost capacity with increased orders from Mr. Roberts. It was a good deal all the way around except for Jack. Neither the parson nor Mr. Roberts had much sympathy for Mr. Maybary. He would just have to fend for himself. This would prove to have drastic consequences as Jack was still the agent of the Devil and the Devil is a poor loser.

CHAPTER THREE

The 1940 Ford

It was now time for Junior to implement his plan for transporting the illegal whiskey from the farm to Bristol. For several months he had been keeping his eye on the car owned by the widow of Tom Webb who used to run the small hardware store down at the crossroads. The car was a 1940 Ford standard coupe. It was popular with salesmen and small businessmen because, while it only had a front seat, it made up for it with an enormous trunk that extended right up to the middle of the body. This gave it a low polar moment of interia even when it was fully loaded.

Junior didn't know a polar moment from the North Pole but he did intuitively understand that a car that had its weight concentrated in the center of the chassis would turn faster and handle better than a car with a lot of overhang. He knew that fast handling of a heavily loaded car was essential for a moonshine car. Overall it was a small car but was built with a reliable V8 engine that lent itself to modification. Junior had been talking with Jerry Price down at Price's garage. Just as Junior had an extraordinary gift for driving, Jerry had a gift for understanding how to get maximum power out of an engine. He also knew how to modify the suspension of the car so it could handle the increased power. Mr. Webb's Ford coupe was about to undergo a remarkable transformation.

Mr. Roberts paid a call on the widow Webb the day after they got back from Bristol. He made her a fair offer of five-hundred dollars on the old Ford which she gladly accepted as she needed money to move in with her sister in Georgia. He told her that his boy got some work in Bristol and thought her well kept car would provide him some reliable, economical transportation. That made the Devil smile. He gave her cash and the car was his.

Junior went down that afternoon and picked up the car after thanking Mrs. Webb and telling her how proud he was to own it and how he would take good care of it. His first stop was at Jerry's garage where he made a deal to have the car extensively modified. This was not Jerry's first conversion of an innocent passenger car to make a whiskey runner. He knew what was needed and he knew how to keep his mouth shut. He also knew to charge a good price. He would order in some special parts and start work first thing next week.

The Roberts' plan was a good one in all respects. But there was one annoyance. They cut Jack off too soon. It was essential that they make a delivery in three days and the car could not be ready that soon. There was no alternative other than to use the car exactly as it was purchased from Mrs. Webb. One delivery would hold them until they could get the car fixed. Pa said he would make the delivery, but Junior wouldn't hear of it. It was his job to drive the car and ready or not he was going to do it. After all the risk was very low. What could happen?

Mr. Webb was a frugal man when he bought the car new in July of 1940. He bought the cheapest version that was sold by Ford. It had a V8 all right but it was the puny 60 horsepower engine that looked lost in the engine compartment. It served its purpose of shuttling a load of nuts and bolts between the warehouse and the store and used a minimal amount of gas in the process. Jerry as his first task would be to yank out the 60 hp engine and replace it with the bigger Mercury engine. But, there it sat for now with the original engine and it was what Junior was going to have drive to Bristol.

Pa and Junior carefully loaded the fifty quarts of shine in the trunk. They packed it in horse blankets and secured it six ways to Sunday with stout ropes. As an extra precaution they also tied the trunk lid shut. Junior waited until it got dark and then started out on the back road. He did not want to venture out onto the state highway, even though it would have saved a lot of time. He knew the back roads like he knew the scriptures that his ma made him memorize.

He felt safe on these deserted roads that were barely two lanes wide. They snaked in and out of the hollows past the small farms like the one he and Pa worked. He knew most of the families from the kids with whom he went to school. They all fought the same hard times. But luck was not with Junior tonight. Unknown to him the revenuers had a tip that Fireball Johnson, a well-known bootlegger, would be coming that way. Fireball was making a run all right but he had gone down the valley route along the river. Two agents were waiting in vain in a 1950 Ford sedan on a side road a half mile from the summit.

Ambushed

The V8 Ford 60 was a pathetic machine. It struggled mightily under the weight of the shine and the pull of gravity as Junior struggled to get up the ridge. At times he had to go down to fifteen miles per hour in first gear to keep the car going. As he neared the summit, he passed the agents drinking their second thermos of coffee while waiting for Fireball to come by. They heard Junior's Ford grinding away as it came up the ridge, its feeble headlights shining in the dark woods. What the hell was this? they thought. What's that old clunker doing out at this time of night? Someone get sick and need the doctor? They went back to the warm coffee as Junior passed.

"Jess, anything look strange to you about that car?" the agent asked.

"Now that you mention it, it is riding awful low in the rear. You don't suppose he's hauling shine do you Phil?'

"I never saw a runner with that sorry a car, but let's check it out. My ass is tired from sitting here anyway. We can say we've done our job and then go home. What do you say Jess?"

"I'm with you. Anything beats just sitting here. Besides that farmer will put out the word that we are around and that may slow things down for a few days."

They pulled the government supplied sedan out onto the road and started to accelerate up the hill toward Junior. It was not going to be much of a challenge to catch the old coupe so they did not use maximum acceleration. Junior was wary even though he was totally inexperienced. He saw the car on the side road but tried to ignore it. He didn't want to create any suspicion. Besides it was probably just a couple of neckers playing stink finger in the back seat. With his sharp vision he saw the car pull onto the road, lights out. He knew he was in big trouble. It was either the cops or a hi-jacker. Either way he was a sitting duck. Junior all but put pressed his foot through the floor board and pounded the steering wheel trying coax one mile per hour more speed out of his overworked motor. It roared but wouldn't go one lick faster. His next thought was to jump out and let the car drop into the valley while he ran into the woods. They would never catch him. But then he quickly considered what failure would mean to the family. The parson would kill the deal and go back to Jack. His ma and pa would go back to hard times. He had to make a run out of it.

It wasn't like a bad dream in slow motion. It was a bad dream in slow motion! He could sense every foot that the pursuit car was gaining on him. They were one turn below and he had 300 feet to reach the summit. Just as they rounded the last curve he crested the summit. Quickly switching off the useless head lights he started gaining speed as the road changed from uphill to downhill. The revenuers saw the lights go off and suddenly realized they had a live one even if he was slow. They turned on the lights shifted down a gear and slammed the gas pedal to the floor. It was only a matter of seconds and they would be on his bumper. From that vantage point they would shoot his tires out. Jess unlimbered his Colt 45 automatic and got ready.

Only sixteen-years-old and in big trouble with the law due to total chance. The Devil didn't play fair. But that's why he is the Devil. In desperation, Junior shifted to second and then to high gear as the coupe rapidly gained speed on the steep downhill grade. He now had the opposite problem to his prior predicament. He had too much speed with insufficient means to control it. The brakes were as pathetic as the engine and the 6.50 -16 Western Auto tires were the bottom of the automotive barrel. Junior jumped the car from side to side on the road as he squealed around the sharp curves devoid of guard rails. He was within inches and milliseconds of death; he would never get closer. The agents backed off since they were paid to catch bootleggers, not get killed racing down the mountain. They only had to wait for the inevitable wreck and pick up the pieces.

Driving by pure instinct, using the slight bit of control he had over the car, Junior whipped the wheel to the left just at the entrance to Swart Hollow road. It was little more than a one lane dirt path scratched out by the county road grader. By some miracle the Ford bounced wildly in the air but stayed on the road. Using what little brakes he had left to broadside the car, Junior came to a halt in a shower of dust and rocks. The left front tire exploded in final protest to the abuse it could no longer tolerate. The feds drove on past the cutoff as they had not seen Junior's violent maneuver. They continued on down the mountain looking for signs of the wreckage that they were sure was there. Not finding any they went home totally puzzled. Junior's legend had started to build at a tender age.

With the invincibility of the young, Junior was not even concerned with his near death. His only concern was how he was going to complete the run to Bristol. He pulled the bald spare tire from behind the seat and put it on the coupe. It would just have to hold until he could replace it. He decided to wait until morning before going back on the road. By that time the car chasing him would have given up. Also he could blend with the farm traffic. There were a lot of 40 Ford coupes still running around the hills and they could serve as decoys. About an hour after dawn he started out again and made it to Bristol without any more trouble. The parson had expected him during the night and was nervous about unloading the trunk during daylight even though they were parked in the closed carriage house. But then who would be suspicious of a young lad like Junior driving an old car?

Junior bought a replacement tire and headed back home, this time using the state highway as he had nothing to hide. What was left of the old motor let the coupe plug along at a sluggish rate of speed. Junior didn't even go home, but parked the car in Jerry's garage.

He never wanted to drive it again as it was now. Jerry gave him a lift home in the wrecker where his frantic mother and anxious dad were waiting for him. He lied a little and said he had car trouble on the way and had to wait until morning to get it fixed. Nothing to worry about now that Jerry was going to change it all anyway. Jerry just smiled and they all went in and had some grits, hog jowl and gravy. When ma wasn't looking Junior slipped pa a big fat envelope. The Devil had lost the first round.

CHAPTER FOUR

Jerry's Garage— and the Makeover

Jerry Price is a bib overalls-wearing, consummate professional. If circumstances had been different he would have been trained as a mechanical engineer and probably worked as a top engine designer in Detroit. He has that kind of intelligence. As it is, he makes a living as a hillbilly mechanic fixing whatever needed fixing. The building of a whiskey runner was a secret release for his awesome, but under-appreciated talent. He is going to build Junior a car the likes of which the mountains had never seen.

He reserved a shed in the back of his garage/junkyard for special projects. No one went in there. He keeps a lock on the door and his junkyard dog chained to a post in front. The first thing he did is pull the body off the chassis and strip the chassis down to a bare frame. Cutting up some eighth inch steel plate he boxed in the frame which greatly increased its strength. He pulled a Columbia two-speed rear end out of a wreck and took it all apart. He made a steel collar to fit over the fracture prone, differential case assembly. It would never break.

He took the brakes off a Lincoln Zephyr and fitted the backing plates to the Columbia. Later he would install the Velvet Touch metallic brake shoes. But first he mounted tubular shock absorbers from a one ton truck to the axle housing so the car had two sets of shocks, the fixed tubular and the adjustable lever style. He also fit a track bar between the pumpkin and the frame. In order to handle the load of moonshine he added extra leaves to the rear spring but kept the arc the same so the car would sit level whether empty or full. Nothing said "bootlegger" louder than a car with a jacked up rear end.

Next he started on the front end. He decided to leave the tube front axle alone. It was both light and strong. A more expensive model would have had an I beam axle to support the larger motor, but this was overkill and Jerry wanted the light axle for fast handling. He did put tube shocks on the front and of course the Lincoln brakes. He also added a stiffer sway bar and stronger springs. The car was going to ride like a lumber wagon when empty but would come into its own when the trunk was loaded. All that was left was the motor and transmission. For the transmission he got a new gear set that fit a Lincoln. He mated the box to an oversize truck clutch working against a light weight Webber steel flywheel.

It was a good thing that Junior had powerful legs. He would need them. His masterpiece was the motor. Starting with a Mercury block he bored it oversize and then welded the crankshaft throws and reground the crank so it would give the engine maximum possible displacement. If this were a race motor he wouldn't have done that, as he could make more horsepower with a shorter crank turning at a higher rpm. But this car would have to have a split personality being as much truck as it was race car. It has a job to do and maximum torque would be required, thus the welded crankshaft.

He had already ordered in special parts from California and they came in by fast express. From Sharp he got aluminum high compression racing heads and a triple carburetor manifold on which he mounted three modified Stromberg 97 carburetors. Jahns sent him forged pistons, four times stronger than stock Ford units. Harmon-Collins provided a modified Scintilla magneto. Ed Iskenderian ground him a special camshaft that would take advantage of the large displacement pistons and free flowing carbs. Fuel economy would suffer but who cared? The name of the game was reliable high horsepower and all compromises were made to achieve this.

Jerry, with his pragmatic understanding of mechanical devices, realized that when manufacturers made piston rings it was impossible for them to be round when installed. They had to have a small slice taken out so they could be expanded to fit around the piston and put in the cylinder bore. Once in the cylinder they would be compressed and the gap would be closed. This meant that the rings were slightly dished on the pistons. This had to effect the operation of the engine. Jerry very cleverly worked out a jig that would close the gap and hone the rings round before they were installed. Thus they formed a perfect circle when installed and the engine would run just a little better. It was subtle tricks like these that made Jerry's engines so special.

The entire engine was assembled with loving care and consummate skill. Gaskets and ports were matched. Valves were triple ground and valve springs were matched to give uniform seat pressure. All rotating assemblies were balanced to perfection. As a final touch Jerry got out his torch and created a set of equal length exhaust headers and attached them to hand rolled, straight through mufflers packed with fiberglass and asbestos. The average hot rod motor could make 175 horsepower. This motor would make well over two-hundred horsepower. With everything assembled Jerry dropped the body backed on the chassis. To the outside world it looked just like Mrs. Webb's old car. The only visual change was a swap to fifteen inch wheels on which were mounted Goodyear "blue dot" police special tires. Junior's car was ready.

When Junior first looked at the car he was disappointed. It looked like the same old slug that almost got him killed. Then Jerry lifted the hood and his sleepy eyes about bulged out of his head. The new motor filled the compartment and aluminum was everywhere. He thoughtfully closed the hood and asked Jerry if it was OK to drive it.

"Go right ahead," said Jerry. "Take it for a run, but bring it back for me to do a final check, and oh yes, be sure to put in 104 octane blue Sunoco gas and only use Sinclair graphite oil."

"I got it," shouted an exuberant Junior. With that he started the engine and put the transmission in first gear. Not knowing what to expect when he let out the clutch he pushed down on the gas like a normal car. The 40 Ford just spun its tires as it took off down the road with the amazed Junior hanging on for dear life. The normally laconic Jerry couldn't stop laughing. Junior headed out onto the highway to play. This was a kid's perfect dream come true. The car responded to him even better than Jack's Oldsmobile. They were literally made for each other. Junior had the strength and quick reactions to handle it and the car had the power and speed that Junior craved.

Since he was still a kid, Junior couldn't resist the challenge offered by a sports car driver coming out of Winston-Salem, driving a

XK140 MC Jaguar roadster. He was wearing string-backed driving gloves and had a sissy golf cap on his head. Quite the fancy dude. He even had a special license plate that spelled LEON. "Well, sir Leon, show me your stuff," Junior thought out loud, "and I will see if I can match it." The Jag shifted down a gear and Junior let him pass. He then kicked the Columbia into high, downshifted to second and glued the Ford to the Jag's tail. In the rear view mirror Junior could see the surprise on Leon's face.

"What the hell is that old Ford doing on my bumper?" Leon thought. "Well, I'll fix that in a hurry." Leon stepped on the gas and the Jag started accelerating under full song. What a beautiful song it was. "So long sucker."

The next time Leon looked back it was to his utter amazement that he saw the Ford still pinned to his bumper, a grinning young kid driving it. This could not be! No kid in an old Ford could match the performance of his magnificent Jaguar sports car with its high output, double overhead cam racing engine. This car was the toast of the continent. What was that mongrel of a Ford doing staying up with it? Now Leon was determined.

The road was starting to get narrow and winding, the Jag was in its element as Leon bore down and drove as hard as he could. He could not believe it when the Ford passed him on a curve and just kept accelerating. The staccato rap of its V8 motor would live in his memory for many years. Then, all of a sudden, the Ford was gone. Junior had ducked off on a side road that Leon did not see. Their paths would cross again many years later, but that is another story.

Junior took the car back to Jerry who gave it a thorough inspection and pronounced it ready for work. Junior paid his bill in cash and headed home. Playtime was over. Time to earn a living.

CHAPTER FIVE

The Midnight Run

With the modified Ford, whiskey delivery was no problem now. They made a special rack to hold the Mason jars securely in place in case of a violent maneuver. Junior was very careful not to constantly take the same route. He had five variations and he rotated between them. A couple of times he was challenged by a pursuit car but he easily outran it. They did not have his driving skill and they couldn't match the performance of Jerry's engine. This made the federal men quite mad. They really didn't know who Junior was or exactly where he came from. They just knew there was a black 1940 Ford coupe that could easily elude them. But a plan was made to catch him.

The feds weren't stupid; they knew the tactics that the runners used including a constant shifting of routes. They figured that it was only a matter of time before Junior repeated a route. To catch him they set up a trap in a narrow cut in the road just beyond the two lane bridge that crossed the river branch. Two cars were positioned out of sight on the shoulder so that they could quickly pull out and make a vee block across the road. A third car hid on a side road about a mile from the bridge. When junior passed by, they would pull out and chase him over the bridge where he would be caught like a rat in a trap. He would either have to stop or die, the choice would be his as there was no way he could get by.

Two days later, Junior started out on a night run with a full load. He decided to take the river road as there might be a little fog down there to hide him. He drove at a steady but not reckless pace. He kept the overdrive in low range and the transmission in third gear. This gave him a 4:11 final drive ratio which was hard on gas mileage but ideal for rapid acceleration if the need arose. About a mile from the river he caught a glimpse of a car on the side road. Looking out his rear view mirror he saw it pull onto the road, lights off. Junior instantly slammed the gas pedal down and started running full blast down the road. When the engine peaked, he let off the gas for a moment and clicked into overdrive at about ninety. The Ford continued to accelerate leaving the chase car behind. The feds' plan was working perfectly. At the entrance to the bridge, Junior's sharp eyes caught the glint of some headlight buckets moving in the bright moonlight. The blocker cars had heard his mufflers blasting and were pulling across the road in vee formation.

With his sharp wits Junior sensed the trap that was laid for him. What happened next is still talked about in the North Carolina hills. Flying onto the bridge at close to 100 miles per hour, Junior yanked on the handbrake locking up the rear wheels so they lost traction. An instant later he jammed on the main brakes and cut the steering wheel hard left. The front wheels retained enough traction to act as a pivot point for the rear end which spun around 180 degrees so the car was facing the other direction in the opposite lane. He then slammed the transmission into second, let off the brakes and stepped full on the gas. The rear tires were lost in smoke as the coupe came to a halt and then started accelerating in the direction from which it had just come. It was Jess, the surprised revenuer, in the chase car that saw Junior coming at him full bore just as he entered the narrow bridge. He had a choice, commit suicide or let Junior go by. He choose the latter. The Devil had lost another round.

As the months went by, Junior became even more expert at delivering the shine. He was never chased again. The money they collected began to bulge in the mattress. They had no worries now. Ma was sick in her heart about the illegal whiskey making as she was a moral, God-fearing woman who recognized the work of the Devil. But she kept her thoughts to herself even though a cold dread is lodged in her heart. Pa is happy for the first time in years, she is feeling back to normal and Junior is not getting into trouble like some other kids in the hills. She really had a lot to be thankful for, but still the bad feeling would not go away.

Junior is getting more adventurous and searching out new outlets for his talented young manhood. One weekend he went with Jerry down to the North Wilksboro speedway to watch the stock cars race. He had never seen a race in his life and is fascinated with the experience. He notices two things right away. First, some of the drivers he knew for sure drove shine cars. In fact, one of the cars was an old runner that was impounded by the sheriff and sold at auction. The other thing he notices, or perhaps more correctly feels, is that he could drive better than those guys on the track. They pay 500 dollars to win the feature race. That could pay for a race car real quick. On the way home Junior makes a deal with Jerry. If Jerry would build him a car to drive he would split the winnings. Jerry likes the idea; he knows that the race cars were below the standard he could build.

So the summer progressed. Jerry built the car and Junior drove it. If he didn't blow a tire or have someone wreck in front of him he won. They were making a little money and having a whole lot of fun. Junior was gaining quite a reputation with the race fans. They would cheer wildly whenever he won. He was also coming to the attention of the government agents who, on their time off, also liked to go to the races. A speculation started to build in their mind about the hill boy who could drive so fast and handle a car so expertly. Hmm!

Jack's Revenge

Jack Maybary was no fool. When the parson's orders started to fall off, he put two and two together and knew he had a competitor. But who? One night he left the boarding house with a cushion under his arm. He sat all night in the park across the street from the church. Just before dawn a 1940 Ford coupe coasted silently into the driveway leading to the carriage house. He could just barely recognize Junior as the driver. So, that was it! He had been double-crossed by Junior and his pa. Well they picked the wrong sucker, Jack thought to himself.

The hill people had a code. If you didn't like what another man was doing, you told him about it straight out. If necessary you used your fists to drive the point home. But you never, never went tattling to the law unless it was a major crime like murder or such. But Jack didn't play by the code. He didn't have the guts. This became clear the day the agents picked him up for selling shine. They caught him taking a payoff from one of his other distributors. Jack was ready to sing like a bird if it would save him from going to prison. The victim of his song would be Junior. He told the feds who he was, where he lived and who he dealt with. They staked out the parson's house and verified Jack's story. They would deal with the parson after they caught Junior.

The agents were actually quite brave and decent men. Most were young college graduates trying to get a start in the Justice Department. Field experience looked good on their record. They had some sympathy for the hill people but they had their job to do and they did it.

One thing they learned the hard way was that you didn't try to bust a still unless you had overwhelming force on your side. The stills were expertly camouflaged and some of the operators were rough old boys. They had been in the war and killed Japs and Nazis who really weren't bothering them all that much. Shooting an agent who was trying to destroy their business and put them in jail would not lay very heavy on their conscience. Pa Roberts was harmless as a fly but they didn't know that and they didn't know for sure where his still was located. If they got Junior they figured his pa would stop making moonshine. They figured right.

The trap they laid was not very clever. It didn't have to be. Junior had to come down one road on every run when he first left the farm. He then had a choice of several routes after that. Because of Jack, they knew the road. They just lay in wait around a sharp curve. They had a tire shredder to string across the road made of sharpened old lawn mower blades. It would destroy all the tires when Junior ran over it. They heard Junior coming and pulled the shredder into place. He was not driving very fast as he had no sense of the imminent danger. This may have saved his life. He rounded the curve and saw the shredder too late to take evasive action. He hit it full on and felt all four Goodyears explode at once. The next thing he knew he was looking down the muzzle of Jess's 45 automatic.

They held the trial in Raleigh where Junior had no reputation to help him or friends on the jury. It wasn't much of a trial as he was stone cold guilty. Because of his age and the fact he had no other offenses the judge took it easy on him. He only gave him two years in the State Penitentiary. Ma and Pa Roberts took it hard. They felt it was all their fault that, in spite of their Christian rearing, they had sinned and deserved punishment more than Junior. Pa destroyed the still and never touched a drop of liquor again. Junior was not too upset. Prison life would not be all that hard on him. He was young and tough and could handle himself. It gave him some time to reflect on his future. Junior did make pa promise to sell the farm and take the money they had saved and buy some good bottom land and grow tobacco. Mr. Roberts did just that. The work of the Devil was still not done. The next round would be Jack's.

A Score is Settled

Jack started working the tractor business in earnest. His days as a moonshine dealer were over. He was a marked man. He bought a new 1952 Oldsmobile convertible and had it painted John Deere bright green. His customers knew it when he pulled into the driveway. The economy was improving and along with it the tractor business. Jack was doing right well by himself. On a trip up to Norton, Virginia, the Devil played his trick. Stanley Cahn had followed Junior's footsteps into the bootleg business. He was now an older, meaner bully, but he still held a grudging respect for Junior. The word had filtered out in the hills that it was Jack who turned in Junior and the parson. In doing so he had broken the number one commandment in the bootlegger's bible. There would be a reckoning.

Stanley was a driver like Junior, except he used a gray Chrysler business coupe equipped with a monstrous hemi engine topped with a supercharger taken off a big diesel truck. It was the most powerful thing on the road even if it didn't handle as well as the lighter Ford. His run took him down the valley from Norton, South to Bristol or North to Charlottesville. He was just coming back in the morning when he spotted Jack ahead of him. The next thing Jack knew he had a big Chrysler banging on his back bumper.

Jack floored the Olds, but even with its four jet carb sucking all the air it could, it was no match for the blown Chrysler. When they got to a sharp curve, Stanley bumped Jack on the left inside bumper and spun him off the curve and down the tree covered bank. The fact that the top was down on the convertible probably saved Jack from more serious injury. Seat belts were unknown then so Jack was thrown into a tree where the branches broke his fall. One arm was broken and his face looked like raw hamburger, but it all healed. The last anyone heard he went back to Iowa and took up school teaching. The Devil had won the final round.

Epilogue

When Junior got out of jail he was a changed young man. He had paid a high price for living the life of a law breaker. While in jail he thought all the time about the racing he did at North Wilksboro. He was good at it and it paid money. He sure didn't want to be a sore-back farmer like his Pa, and now he had a prison record to worry about. He made tracks straight for Jerry's garage to see what Jerry was doing. Jerry didn't want to be a small town mechanic any more than Junior wanted to be a farmer. They formed a race team and started touring the Southeastern bull rings. They were good and they won. They also got caught up by progress when NASCAR was formed and racing went big time with corporate sponsors and television. The Price and Roberts Racing Team gained national fame and they became wealthy men.

Some members of the racing fraternity who knew Junior during his early days as a driver sometimes catch a glimpse of him standing with one leg on the pit wall during rather monotonous mid-race laps. His sleepy eyes are still hidden under bushy lashes and the usual benign expression is on his face. The powerful body now wears a layer of late middle age fat that fills out the colorful racing attire that he wears. Maybe his still razor sharp mind is concentrating on the strategy for the next pit stop or perhaps critically evaluating his young driver's performance. But then it may be that he is thinking back to the days when as a young, reckless youth he was in his Ford coupe racing through a deserted hollow on his way to Bristol.

To Continue Reading . . .
Please visit www.CharleSClarkAuthor.com

Charles S. Clark is a retired professional medical electronics engineer. He earned a BS in Biology from Union College in Schenectady, NY and an EE from Cornell Univesity, Ithaca, NY. An entrepreneur, he is founder of Sandhill Scientific who has had a lifelong love affair with old cars starting with his 1940 Ford coupe purchased in 1954 for $500. He has spent years repairing and assembling old flatheads and designing and building new fuel injection systems for that old Ford engine.

Charles is currently the proud owner of many old cars—including the 1940 Ford Standard coupe featured in *The Bootlegger '40 Ford,* a 1940 Lincoln Continental convertible and 1955 Chrysler 300. Along the way, he has owned and restored Corvettes, Mustangs, Pontiac GTOs, and Camaros. He even shared ownership of a 1948 Pontiac he bought for $75, then traded it for a 1950 Olds Holiday hardtop!

As an octogenarian, he doesn't muse about the past. Rather, Charles puts the hammer down and roars through into the future.

Printed by Libri Plureos GmbH in Hamburg, Germany